LIFE'S A WITCH
THE WITCHES OF BROOME HILL

SIMONE NATALIE

*For my family, who are more magical
and chaotic than any character
I could think up.*

Life's a witch

I am far too kind, and that's the problem.

I was far too kind as a child, when, over and over again, I let my older sister have her way when she wanted to play the witch, leaving me to play the boring human.

I was far too kind as a teen, when I took over my grandmother's shop of oddities and witchcraft so that she could go off and teach young witches how to build gingerbread houses. Leaving me here for years and years.

I was too kind when I turned my ex into a frog. He deserved so much more than that for what he put me through. I was even kind enough to find a home for him when I couldn't remember how to turn him back.

And I was definitely too kind when I agreed to apprentice my nephew at the shoppe, so that he could put it down as work experience on his University of Wizardry and Witchcraft application.

Far too kind.

Because, if I hadn't done that, I wouldn't be in this huge mess right now!

Chapter 1

'I'm going to need you to explain exactly what happened last night,' I said firmly, putting on my most serious 'Aunt' voice.

'Well,' began Morgan, my thirteen-year-old nephew. 'It was late last night. I was closing up like you asked me to, when in barged a customer. She was crying and pleaded with me to sell her a potion. I know you said no dark potions, but—'

'I didn't say no dark potions *at all*, Morgan,' I cried, cutting him off. 'I told you no commissions at all without my prior approval! There are bad people out there and it's dangerous to make bargains with them.'

'I know, dark magic, eternity in hell, blah blah blah,' he replied. 'Mum already warned me. But this woman didn't look evil. Actually, she just looked kind of sad.' He spoke flippantly as he spun back and forth on the kitchen stool. 'She was at least as old as Granny and dressed up like she'd come straight off the early emo scene.' He stopped spinning and gave me a meaningful look. 'You know, all chunky silver belts, hair dyed pink and black, with a huge fringe. You *know* the look.' I was starting to feel like perhaps Morgan had gotten into a box of my old photos and was now trying to not-so-subtly shame me for my teenage-style choices.

'She had mascara running all down her face and a bubble of snot just hanging…' He pointed to his nose and made a gagging motion.

Yeah, this kid had no sympathy for anyone.

'But, most importantly,' Morgan continued, 'she had a *huge* bag of gold coins. I checked them, Aunty, and I swear they are all real.'

I shook my head in frustration.

'Look, Morgan, what is my one golden rule?' My nephew rolled his eyes up to the dusty ceiling and shoved the rest of his breakfast, a blueberry muffin, into his mouth. 'Do as I say, not as I do,' I continued, as he mimicked along.

'I know,' he said. 'But you need the money, Aunty H. I know you hate it here. It's about damn time you hired some witch to look after it, so that you can go out and do what you want for a change.'

I had to admit, I felt a little touched that he had thought of me. He may act like a no-good ruffian, but…

'Besides,' he went on, 'if you didn't want me to sell love potions, then why did you already have one in the safe?' All sense of tenderness withered away to pure panic at that moment.

'Morgan, please tell me you didn't give that woman a love potion.'

He stood up from the kitchen table and pulled his school jumper on over his head, looking completely unfazed, and fished out a crumpled piece of paper from his pocket. He held it out to me.

'Here is the receipt. I put the gold coins in the till, all two hundred of them.' He smirked proudly.

'Two hundred?!' I stammered. 'You sold a love potion… one of *my* love potions, for two hundred coins? The fact you sold it at all is bad enough, but it is worth a lot more than that, Morgan!' I admonished. 'You are SO lucky that I put an expiry on all of my mind-altering spells. Could you imagine if she cursed some poor person to love her for life?'

'I'm concerned by how much this is upsetting you, Aunty H,' said Morgan. 'It's done, chill out. I'm sure she just wanted to spell some lonely neighbour.'

In the three weeks that Morgan had been helping me, he had seen me do plenty of morally grey things. I couldn't count the amount of times I had warned him 'Do not tell your mother'. This was on another level, however. Love potions were highly illegal, and for good reason.

SIMONE NATALIE

Even if I *had* planned to sell the love potion one day, I would have taken great care in checking whom it went to. I certainly wouldn't have sold it to any random teary witch with a bag full of money. Transactions like that needed to be monitored closely, not passed off to any witch that stumbled through the door. If it fell into the wrong hands, a love potion could be incredibly dangerous, and an untrustworthy customer could point the finger back to me.

I paced the room, suddenly feeling a little claustrophobic. Morgan watched me cautiously from behind his glasses, his messy blonde curls, so similar to my own, stuck up on end from the static of his school jumper.

'Have I really messed up?' he asked quietly, beginning to realise the gravity of his error.

I stopped pacing and shook my head as I flattened his hair down nervously.

'Probably not, kiddo,' I reassured him. 'I expect she was just lonely, as you said. The potion will only last for one night, anyway. So no matter. It may already be done.' I pulled his schoolbag from the back of one of the kitchen chairs and handed it to him.

'Get yourself to school. I'll see you tonight,' I said. He nodded and threw the bag over his shoulder.

'And Morgan?' I added as he slipped his feet into his shoes, ready to leave the shoppe. 'Don't tell your mum.'

LIFE'S A WITCH

He smiled weakly and disappeared out into the street. I waited for Bell to stop ringing, a sign that the coast was clear, and hurriedly locked the door, turning the sign over to 'Closed'.

I had run this shoppe now for ten years, and managed to somehow keep out of any serious trouble in all of that time.

My parents died when I was in my infancy, and my grandmother took me and my older sister in and raised us. She was a powerful, famous witch. Centuries old.

While she looked after us, she led as stable a life as a witch like her could lead. However, the moment I turned eighteen, the sisterhood came calling for her, and I couldn't hold her back any longer.

This shoppe had been the site of our covenstead for thousands of years. Before it was made from bricks and mortar, it was made of flint, and before that it was a hut, and before that a mound of earth with a ley line running through.

This sacred ground was in our blood, so one of us had to take it.

Any coven member could have done it, really. However, my mother had been high priestess, and the coven wanted one of us.

My older sister, Raven, went running for the hills as soon as Granny announced she was leaving. Raven lived a human life, away from the upheaval and chaos expected of magic. She was a police officer, and a divorcee single mother.

SIMONE NATALIE

It suited her, and she was happy. Except that her only son, Morgan, came into his powers extraordinarily young. Four years before initiation age, he could cast spells; and now, on the verge of fourteen, he was being sought after by the world of magic, and universities and covens alike wanted to train him.

He was still just a kid, though, with so much to learn. He was still naïve.

Had I failed him by setting a bad example? Had he seen me selling illegal spells and thought it was normal?

I pulled down the window shutters and stepped through into the back room, where my safe was concealed behind a hand-stitched tapestry. It depicted my grandmother defeating a Cerberus in a fairly bloody battle. In actuality, the dog had been her pet for many years. She enjoyed posing for artwork like this – that is, until the Cerberus ate a coven member, then it was back to the underworld with it.

I ran my hands over the safe, letting my magic crackle from my fingertips. The metal door swung open at my touch.

Inside were countless jars and parcels, of all shapes and sizes, some filled with dried herbs, flowers, or long-extinct creatures, and some with potions. Spiderwort, Essence of Insanity, Dragon Fang... There were potions that were complete, potions that were incomplete, and some that were made for mixing. There were powdered, liquid and gas potions. Almost anything a witch could want.

LIFE'S A WITCH

I was immensely proud of my collection.

I checked over the jars, running my fingers along the lids and labels. It was clear that the love potion was gone.

So it was true. Morgan had somehow gained access to my safe, and sold that potion.

I don't know how he did it, but he did.

I needed to change the lock spell, but for now a simple alarm spell would have to suffice.

I shut the door and took my athame, the ceremonial dagger that had once belonged to my father, from its sheath hidden under my jumper. I waved it over the tapestry, whispering my intent, and felt the familiar tingle of magic in the air.

'*Slán*,' I breathed. 'Keep it safe.'

Once done, I went back to the shoppe, opened the shutters and flipped the sign back.

It was drizzling out now. I smiled to myself as I breathed in deeply, taking in the crisp October air, but then my nose bristled.

'Hmm.'

There was something dark out there today.

I frowned and, opening the door, scanned the wet cobblestoned street, watching shoppers rush around under their umbrellas as they dashed into shop doors. I couldn't see anything untoward. But I could feel it.

I quickly stepped back into the shoppe, shutting the door behind me. I gripped my athame from inside my jumper for a moment, alarmed. It glowed warmly at my touch. I looked up at the doorway, to see that Bell was still, silent, and unconcerned. Which was reassurance enough.

'No matter,' I said aloud to no one in particular. 'I'll pop the kettle on and get to restocking the felt witch hats.'

Chapter 2

Later that day, I was busy cutting open a new arrival of jelly worms, when the little bell above my shoppe door suddenly rang out from the next room. I jumped up in alarm from behind the pile of boxes.

Instead of its usual gentle chime, Bell was ringing out erratically in warning, as if it was trying to hop down from its spot atop the door frame.

Not good.

I went to the front of the shoppe to investigate, and immediately my stomach churned in panic as I spotted our guest. The person was tall and graceful, with long, pitch-black hair tied neatly at the base of their neck. The figure wore plain, black clothes with no patterns or shape, giving them an androgynous look.

The air in the room seemed to still completely. Even the dust paused mid-air in its aimless flurry, as though time itself had stopped.

The person's frame filled the entire doorway, spread out like some elegant creature that was far too large for the shoppe. However, they stepped in with ease, flicking the excitable Bell playfully with a long, bejewelled finger as they slipped past.

The visitor met my eyes and all my senses flared in alert and screamed 'danger'. No wonder Bell was freaking out. Everything about this person was spiderlike. Their face was angular and sharp, almost inhuman in its beauty, with irises of ruby red staring intensely from kohl-lined eyes.

'What is a vampire doing in my little spell shoppe?' I asked, trying to keep my voice steady.

The vampire smiled a wide, wicked grin, that made the pit of my stomach swoop.

'I am here to see you, of course.' Their voice was low, masculine and lyrical. I shivered.

'Why would that be?' I asked, as I took an involuntary step backwards. The vampire smiled again, and shut the door behind him before casually flipping the sign that hung there, from 'Open' to 'Closed'.

'I'm slightly hurt that you don't already know. But perhaps I overestimated you, witch.'

LIFE'S A WITCH

'If you thought of me at all, then you have overestimated me,' I said, with a nervous laugh. I stepped away again, the back of my legs bashing clumsily into the counter, and my till popped open with an excitable 'ding'. I fumbled for a moment, trying my hardest to press the panic button without the vampire noticing.

'And what good would that do, witch?' he asked, obviously realising my intentions. 'Who would come? The city guards? The human Police? I don't think they would interfere with royal business.'

'Royal business?' I asked, feeling sick. There were only two royal vampires in this part of England, and I didn't want to get involved with either of them. Surely the King from the Court of Roses wouldn't come in person to my little shoppe? So, who was this? It could be his son?

'If they did come,' continued the vampire, as he walked around the room, showing feigned interest in my pots of luck, shimmer dust and novelty wands, 'I have a feeling they would be on my side. It's not very often a witch of no circumstance manages to bespell a vampire prince. I am sure they would be *very* interested in hearing how you did it. Love potions are outlawed now, aren't they?'

Oh shit. Double shit.

'Vampire prince? I am honoured,' I said. 'What's the protocol here? Do I curtsy?' I laughed again, but quickly cut off with a weird choke as the vampire was suddenly standing face to face with me. It happened in a blink – one moment he was inspecting the wax fingers, the next he was pressing in on me, towering over me. His long fingers gripped my chin, hard, and roughly pulled my face right up so that I had no choice but to meet his crimson eyes.

'Hi,' I said, nervously. He didn't look amused. His cruel mouth was a tight, thin line.

'Hi,' he breathed back, the tone of his voice dripping like poisoned honey. 'Care to explain?'

For a moment, I couldn't find my voice. My heart was pounding in my chest and all I could think about was how warm the visitor was. Weren't vampires supposed to be cold? I had never met one in person before.

'Uh, here's the thing,' I began, my voice coming out in a meek croak. 'I never sell love potions usually, but she looked so lonely, and I felt sorry for her. I thought she would spell her little old neighbour or something. I had no idea it was for you.' This all came out in a tumble of word-vomit, I knew how feeble it sounded, but there was no way I would mention Morgan, or his part in it.

'I'm not sure what you know about vampires, witch, but we don't like to be lied to.' He splayed his fingers along my jaw and I shivered at the mixed sensations of fear and excitement.

LIFE'S A WITCH

I should have known that no good would come from taking on an apprentice. When we were young my sister was always getting me into trouble, It was no surprise that her son would do the same.

What was I supposed to do now? I couldn't tell this vampire the truth, but he would know a lie.

'Fine,' I snapped, as adrenalin flooded my veins. 'She was a weird old lady,' I continued, 'with a very large bag of coins and I *needed* those coins. It's true that I had no idea it would be you. I mean, surely, this is as much your fault as it is mine? How the hell did she get close enough to poison your drink with my potion, anyway? You're a prince, surely you wouldn't be stupid enough to drink something gifted from a complete rando?'

I was breathless after that. My chest was heaving as I gasped for air, and I couldn't really remember what I had said. However, the vampire was laughing heartily, so either it was really good, or *really* bad.

He let go of me and stepped away. It felt like a weight was being lifted.

'I didn't expect that "rando", as you called her, to have a strong love potion on her person,' he said. 'Poison I can handle easily, curses and hex bags are nothing to me. But I have never seen anything like your love potion. We are all very lucky that it wasn't strong enough to hold me for more than a day.'

'It most certainly was strong enough,' I bulked. 'I set a timer on it. I may have sold out for money, but I'm not cruel enough to bespell someone for ever – at least, not someone who has done me no harm,' I added, thinking of Josh, my ex-boyfriend turned swamp-inhabiting frog.

'So, you mean to tell me,' the vampire continued, 'that you have the power to make someone fall completely in love with whomever you so wish, even someone like me, for any determinable amount of time?'

I shrugged. 'I suppose I must have,' I said.

He laughed then, in a way that could only be described as devious. It stretched on a bit, so I laughed nervously with him as I slowly backed away into the store room and quickly locked the door behind me.

'What a psycho,' I mumbled as I slid down to the soft, carpeted floor. The door was spelled, so hopefully the vampire wouldn't be able to break through. I couldn't stay in this little room for ever though, could I? Sure, there were jars of edible things, but edible didn't mean I should eat them, and that wouldn't last long, anyway. Besides, vampires lived forever, right? They were immortal, so would he just wait out there for me to get bored?

'This carpet of yours is very interesting.'

My mouth opened in a silent scream, and my neck snapped to the side so fast that it made an unpleasant noise in protest. The vampire was sitting on the floor next to me, his back against the same old, wooden door that mine was against. He was running his elegant fingers along the carpet, and staring down at it in what seemed like genuine revere.

'Very witchy.' He continued, seemingly oblivious to my reaction. 'Is it spelled?' He asked.

I shook my head in bewilderment. How on earth had he gotten in here, and sat down next to me without my noticing?

'It's just…old' I answered vaguely.

'Well, it is lovely.'

'Thanks.'

'You're welcome.' He looked at me then, with a knowing smirk.

I groaned in frustration, this vampire was not going to back down and leave me alone, was he?

'Okay' I said, sitting up straighter. 'Let's skip the small talk. What do I have to do to make up for this?' I asked, earnestly. 'What do I have to do for you to walk out of this shoppe and never come back?'

'You could pay in blood?' He smiled widely and ran his tongue over one of his long, white fangs. It was weirdly seductive, but I had no interest in becoming food.

'Next?'

'Make me another potion,' he said, all humour dropping from his face. 'Make me a potion as strong as the one you made for the granny, and make it last for the span of three full moons.'

'Then we will be even?' I asked, cautiously. He smiled again, a wicked side grin that made me squirm.

'We won't ever be even, witch.'

'Why should I do it, then?' I demanded in exasperation. 'What incentive is that?'

'I probably won't kill you if you do me this *favour*,' he said, deadpan.

'I know I'm in no position to bargain, but I think there is a bit too much leeway with that,' I mumbled.

He rubbed his chin dramatically, as if to consider this.

'Perhaps,' he agreed. 'Fine, you will make me the potion. And, if it works exactly as I wish it to, then I will set you free and never bother you, or your kin, for as long as I live.' He looked at me seriously again then, his red eyes staring into my soul as if he could see everything hidden there. 'However, if it doesn't work, you will be indebted to me, and at my beck and call, for as long as I live.'

I swallowed hard. 'So, if it works, I will be completely free from you?' I asked.

'It will be as I said.'

'And you can't add any sneaky stipulations into the bargain. It has to be a simple love spell, that runs for the span of three full moons,' I confirmed.

He nodded his elegant head. 'It must work.'

LIFE'S A WITCH

I smiled genuinely and held my hand out to him. 'You have a deal,' I said. 'My spells always work.'

'So confident,' he said, clicking his tongue in approval. It was a bit mesmerising, actually.

The vampire took my hand in his much larger one and shook it. Then, quick as a flash, he pulled me in closer and nipped the skin at the base of my thumb. And, before I could protest, he took my thumb to his mouth and licked the blood there.

'All debts should be in blood,' he said in response to my look of horror. He let me go and I cradled my hand in shock. When I inspected my thumb, there was no mark, and it didn't hurt when I pressed it.

'What's your name, witch?' he asked pleasantly, as though nothing bloodthirsty had just happened.

'Hedgehog,' I replied steadily.

He stared at me for a heartbeat, his face blank.

'No, really?' he asked, his mouth lifting into a smirk.

'Really, that's my name,' I said calmly.

'Did your parents hate you?' he spluttered, looking a little less inhuman. 'I am not calling you that,' he insisted. He shook his head in bewilderment. 'Is it really Hedgehog?'

'Yes!' I insisted, feeling pretty insulted now. 'You're a vampire, can't you tell the difference between the truth and a lie?'

'Well, I'm not calling you that,' he repeated. 'I'll call you Hedge… or Hog, maybe.'

'You will not,' I replied, darkly.

'I'll call you whatever I want, pig-witch,' the vampire said, with a large, playful smile that softened his face. My stomach did a little swoop, and I quickly stood up and stepped away. He looked bemused, as if he found my reaction comical.

'You are cute, for a witch.'

'Call me cute, or hog, or pig-witch one more time, and then we will see how cute you find me,' I threatened. This made him happier still, and I could tell the more I protested the more he would enjoy it.

'My potion recipes are a secret, so you need to leave now,' I said, in as commanding a voice as I could muster when faced with a creature like this.

'Family recipe?' he asked, with his smirking side smile.

'Something like that, yes.'

'Very well.' He stood up and brushed down his clothes, which were now covered in a layer of crystalline, glittering dust from the store room carpet he had so admired. I felt a little bit of satisfaction when he struggled to get it all off.

'Vampires shouldn't sparkle like this,' he said in frustration.

'I think it suits you,' I said, sniggering.

'One more thing, before I go,' the vampire said, as he pushed open the door, the lock spell seemingly void as far as he was concerned.

'Hmm?' I prompted.

'I want the carpet.'

Chapter 3

Once I was sure that the vampire had left, I burnt down two full bundles of sage to cleanse the energy. I was careful to cover every area in my shoppe that he may have touched. When I had finished, I went to the door and administered a rub of strong whisky to Bell's bronze lip, to calm her clanging nerves.

Looking out of the window, I could see that the sun was setting behind the treeline, and the high street shoppers were beginning to withdraw. I nodded politely to other shop staff across the way, as they began to close up for the evening.

The street lamps and display window lights were lit, casting a hazy glow on the world. Halloween and Samhain decorations coloured the doorways and pathways in orange and yellow. I could hear the church bells at the centre of town ringing out the hour.

SIMONE NATALIE

My nerves were rattled, but I had to centre myself. I was expecting visitors and they would be able to tell that something was wrong. There was nothing so meddlesome as a witch in situations like this.

Tonight, the moon was waning gibbous, and my coven would be gathering together to begin the celebrations of Samhain. The shoppe, as our covenstead, was the meeting place.

There were only twelve active members of our coven left in town, as most were in the wind. Witches were prone to wondering. We needed to learn new techniques, meet new people, settle in new towns and teach other witches. It was how we kept our craft alive.

Centuries ago, my bloodline had been known and feared throughout the world as the Witches Of Broome. However, we simply went by the name of Caelum these days. Our numbers were beginning to fade with the emergence of newer, more popular covens, and Caelum sounded a bit more modern and *witchy*.

My grandmother had hated the name change. However, it had worked for a time, as we now welcomed at least one new member a year, and had a popular social media following. I left all of that to Morgan, though.

My role was to be high priestess of our coven, the highest role a witch could have within their circle.

LIFE'S A WITCH

My mother and grandmother had both been high priestess in their time, so it was natural that, once I took over the shoppe, I would take over and lead the coven.

It was in my blood. I was rooted to this coven, as surely as I was rooted to this ancestral home here on the hill.

As high priestess, I would lead the coven meeting tonight. It was called a circle meeting, because it was carried out within a protective magic circle, where outside influence and dark magic could not enter. It was a safe space to work magic.

I stepped away from the window, leaving the door unlocked and under the constant watch of the enchanted bell. I walked through the shoppe and made my way down to the basement of the building, where our circles were always held.

I prepared the room, drawing over lines that had been marked out in pen, chalk, water and fire countless times before. I then lit five white candles, to signify the five elements: spirit, air, fire, water and earth.

Bell rang out from above and, one by one, my coven arrived, shuffling down the old wooden steps, dressed already in their ceremonial robes. It was an outfit choice that was a little more acceptable this close to Samhain, as the humans just presumed we were on our way to a costume party, dressed up as old wizards, or characters from *The Lord of the Rings*.

'Blessed be,' I greeted happily as each person arrived. Some brought cake or jars of preserves as gifts.

'I made you a pumpkin tart!' Cole O'Mara announced as he made his way down the steps.

'Goddess preserve us,' whispered Mary, the oldest member of the coven, who arrived just before him. I couldn't blame her; Cole was kind hearted, but his baking was something truly devious.

Cole was only a few years older than me, and had dated my sister for a time when we were teens. Raven had ended it with him because she thought he was only dating her to get close to me. However, it had been about fifteen years since then and he had never made a move, or been anything other than friendly.

He placed the tart down on a table with the other gifts, and joined his place in the circle. He gave me a friendly wink and I rolled my eyes, as I always did when he winked at me, or flirted playfully.

More people arrived, and for a while the room was filled with merrymaking, hugging and cries of 'Blessed be'.

'Welcome, Caelum!' I said, when everyone had settled down.

'Blessed be,' they all chanted in unison.

'With Samhain getting closer, I want to start this week's circle by thinking about new beginnings,' I began. 'With this season comes many changes. With the death of the old, it's a good time to start thinking about what we want to leave behind us, and what we want to take with us into next year.'

'I want to leave my arthritis behind,' cackled Mary.

'Me too,' chimed in Doris beside her.

'I think tonight we should take some time to focus on the things that might be holding us back,' I said, 'and how we can overcome them.'

'I have been feeling a dark presence lately,' said Hazel, one of our newest members. She was only just initiated, and had joined up with her mother, Vera. 'It's been holding me back, because I am too scared to leave the house.'

Mary rolled her eyes at this. I shook my head at her, reproachfully.

'She won't even go to school!' Vera added, sounding worried.

'Then we will add some healing and ward-evil chants to our circle,' I said kindly.

Everyone sat down, cross-legged, in the half-drawn circle that I had already marked out. I lit more candles at the points of the pentagram and then finished off the circle in chalk, closing it against the outside world.

We meditated for a while, all focusing on our own worries and fears. I tried not to think about the vampire and how immoral I was being by helping him.

After a while, I went around the room, asking each person what they wanted to achieve this month, and what they needed help with.

SIMONE NATALIE

I was the only member of my family here, as my sister hadn't been to a circle meeting in years, and Morgan was still too young.

A young teenage witch, named Heidi, shared that she was fighting with her boyfriend, as he didn't want her practising witchcraft anymore. She asked the goddess for guidance and patience. I would have told her that she didn't need a controlling person like that in her life, but as high priestess I had to be neutral, even if it was a neutral chaos.

Mary wanted help with her garden. She was growing an unseemly amount of deadly nightshade 'just in case', and her neighbours were lodging complaints against her.

It was a typical circle, but about halfway through I could tell something was wrong.

The candles I had lit to signify the five elements were flickering wildly, and some were going out completely.

The atmosphere felt off. I tried to ignore it, but when it came to my time to share, I found I couldn't talk. My throat felt tight, as if it was closing up.

I coughed and sputtered until my breath became a gasp.

The witch next to me, a woman about my age named Fiona, acted quickly by rubbing away the chalk lines and breaking the circle. I felt relief instantly.

I gasped out my thanks to her, as I began to breathe more clearly the moment the circle was open. I stood up shakily, and Cole rushed forwards to help me. I waved him away and gave him a reassuring smile.

I looked up to see eleven very concerned faces staring back at me. I felt instantly guilty, my worries had tainted the circle and caused dark energy to spill into our safe space.

'You in trouble then?' asked Mary.

'Just a bit,' I croaked out. 'Nothing I can't handle.'

'Well, it's clear you don't want to share, so I won't ask you, too,' she continued. 'Give me some hair, and I will bury it.'

I shook my head vehemently. I was weary, always, of giving something like that freely. Even for a protection spell.

'Very well,' said Mary with a shrug. 'Suit yourself.'

'We should disband now,' I said. 'I don't think it's going to get much better than this.' A few people chuckled nervously.

We packed up and blew out the last of the candles. As the coven members trickled out into the cold, dark night, a few of them wished me luck, a few more frowned and shook their heads at me.

I had ruined the circle by hiding important truths from them, so I couldn't be mad that they were disappointed.

Part of me wondered, then, if I should have asked them for help or advice, but I was too embarrassed to have landed myself in this situation.

More than that, I didn't want to involve Morgan, and if I didn't tell all of the truth, they would sense it.

I locked the door behind my coven and let out a long exhalation of relief.

I probably didn't need to be so worried.

The vampire had promised to leave me be as long as he got what he wanted, and I had no reason to suspect that he would go back on that.

I pulled all of the shutters down over the windows, the noise seeming to echo in every corner of my home.

Once the shoppe was plunged into darkness, I pulled the hood up on my ceremonial robe and shut my eyes. Slowly, calmly, I relaxed my body and let my magic unwind. It flowed through my veins, up my arms and through to my fingertips.

'Shed a little light. Éadrom.' Instantly, every candlewick in the room flared, emitting a soft, golden glow. The fireplace behind my counter blazed up, crackling and spluttering as it consumed the stacks of wood I had placed there earlier.

Glittering dust danced in the air, illuminated by the glow. It flurried around, pulsing and swaying, some of it landing on the termite-ridden shelves.

I ran my bare hands over those shelves, gathering the magic until my fingers were coated in the thick webs of the dust. Then, I transferred it to the edge of my athame.

I walked over to my cauldron that hovered over the fireplace and, with a quick flick of my wrist, sent the dust cascading into it.

To a large glass jar, I added a spoonful of bespelled water, a sprinkle of dried herbs, an elixir of dandelion, a sprig of lavender, three mustard seeds and a squeeze of lemon.

LIFE'S A WITCH

I sealed the jar, shook it and then placed it inside my large black cauldron, where it lay on top of the shimmering dust.

It sizzled and hissed until the overheated glass eventually cracked, smashing into pieces with a satisfying tinkle. I used a pestle to grind together the mixture of potion and glass, and added to the concoction a pre-made liquid potion, to bring about affection. This is where I would usually say the words of power, but I felt uneasy. The love potion had to be the strongest one I had ever made. There was no room for mistakes here.

I had to have a guarantee, and I knew just the thing for it.

I raced to my safe in the back room and searched through the jars and parcels stored there until I found what I was looking for.

A tiny jar of thick, pink liquid. Enough to fill a thimble.

There was a label attached to the cork, in tiny, scribbled handwriting. It said 'Go ciallmhar'.

It was in case of emergency, to be used wisely.

This potion had belonged to my mother. She had brewed it herself when I was only a child. I'm not sure what she had planned it for, but I felt that the looming possibility of becoming enslaved by a vampire prince would definitely constitute an emergency.

I hesitated for a moment before I let a tiny drop slip from the rim of the glass vial and into my potion. I didn't really know what the spell consisted of, but most of what made a spell work a certain way was the intent behind it, and my intention was to make sure the vampire prince got what he needed.

The potion sizzled and turned a beautiful shade of pink. I took my wooden ladle from its hook and spooned the concoction into an empty glass vial. I stoppered it with a cork and a seal of green dyed wax.

I whispered the words of power as I ran my athame over the top. When I felt satisfied, I pressed the warm glass to my lips in a quick kiss, just for good measure.

Now, I needed to charge it under moonlight for one night, and it would be ready.

Chapter 4

The vampire prince came for me two days later, while Morgan and I were seated at the table eating breakfast.

Morgan's spoon, piled high with cereal, was halfway to his mouth when he suddenly let go of it, the spoon falling down into the bowl with a loud clatter. I looked up to find Morgan staring at me, his face pale, frozen in horror.

'Something's coming,' he said, his voice cracking, and not just in the usual teenage-boy way.

I didn't waste any time doubting him. Wordlessly, I gathered up his school things and handed them to him. Then I took hold of his arm and pulled him out of his chair. I didn't want him anywhere near here when the vampire arrived.

'Time to get to school, kid. You need to go down the fire escape,' I told him, leading him upstairs. He followed shakily.

I didn't know what he could sense, or see, but it had rattled him to his core.

As we got to the window in my room, I heard Bell jangling loudly from the shoppe door below. Morgan looked at me, his pale blue eyes wide in fright.

'Someone's here,' he mouthed.

'Don't worry, it's fine,' I whispered, trying to be casual. 'This is nothing I can't handle.'

He shook his head. 'I can't leave you.'

'Oh yes you can, kid!' I half pushed, half carried him out of the window and onto the metal ladder below.

'You would only get in the way,' I added. 'I'll see you after school!' As I said that, my voice faltered, but I slammed shut the window quickly before he could notice.

Morgan stood at the top of the ladder for a moment, staring at me, unsure and concerned. But I smiled and waved him away impatiently. I watched him until he had descended. I saw him hesitate a moment, before hoisting his bag up on his back and walking down the street and out of view.

I took a large, calming breath before I went back down.

The vampire was sitting at the table, in Morgan's vacated chair. He had pushed the bowl of cereal away in disgust and had his feet up in its place, resting lazily on the scuffed oak wood of the table. He looked relaxed, at ease.

In complete contrast, I could feel the room around him reacting to his presence. His other-ness thumped and pulsed in the air, and set my nerves on edge.

'Good morning, dear Hodge,' he greeted.

Hodge? Was that a mix between Hedge and Hog? Urgh.

'Didn't anyone ever teach you how rude that is?' I asked, nodding at his feet and ignoring his new nickname for me.

The vampire smiled. 'Rude to whom? I expect that I grew up with a different set of etiquette rules to you.' I had forgotten how effecting the sound of his voice was. It wasn't something a person could recall with any real accuracy. It was low, yet light and lyrical all at the same time. I could feel it reverb in my chest.

'Well, vampire prince, you are in my home now, so I think you should follow *my* rules,' I replied.

The vampire sat up and stared me down for a moment, his sharp face unreadable. After a time, he silently removed his legs from the table, one polished black boot after the other.

'Call me Heston,' he said, splaying his hands out on the table. 'I have to admit, I do admire that ability of yours,' he added, eyeing me curiously.

'What ability?' I asked.

'The very admirable ability to speak out *so* confidently against me, when I can hear and feel how fast your tiny little heart is beating in fear of me.'

I didn't know how to reply, so I slowly sunk into the seat opposite him instead. I hadn't wanted to give him the satisfaction of seeing me rattled, so it was frustrating and unnerving to know that he could already tell.

'You have my potion?' he asked as he watched me. He looked like a predator stalking its prey, all small pupils and intense looks, locked onto every movement and twitch I made.

I pulled the love potion from the inner pocket of my dress and slid it across the table to him. He looked at it for a moment before smiling softly.

'Perfect,' he breathed.

'Are we done now?' I asked, hopefully. 'I have a lot to do and you are upsetting the balance of my shoppe.'

'We are not done, dear Hodge. Not until the spell has run its course.'

'That's three full months!' I cried, jumping up from my seat. 'Our bargain was—'

'Our bargain was for you to make me a potion that worked for the course of three full moons. Did you think I wouldn't take you with me?' He laughed humourlessly. 'I need some kind of collateral. What is to stop you giving me a fake potion and then running off?'

'Why would I do that?' I snapped 'I live here. I have always lived here and I am *not* leaving.' I folded my arms and shot him the most withering glare I could muster, which probably looked more like begging than anything else.

LIFE'S A WITCH

The vampire prince stared pointedly at Morgan's cereal bowl, and then flicked his eyes back to meet mine.

'You do not have to go,' he breathed, poisonously. 'I could take another in your stead?' The wave of fear that hit my stomach made me feel sick. The hairs on my arms stood on end. The vampire smiled wide, clearly knowing the effect his words had on me.

'When do we leave, vampire?' I asked, defeated.

'Please, call me Heston.' He rose gracefully from the chair and held a hand out to me. 'We leave now.'

'I need to pack…' I began to argue, but the look he gave me was firm and dark.

'I have people I cannot just abandon,' I said.

'You may write a note,' he said, pulling a flame-licked scroll from the nearest shelf. He handed it to me, along with a quill from his breast pocket.

'Keep it short,' he commanded. 'And don't worry about packing. You will have everything you need.'

I wrote a note to my sister.

Raven,
I am in the wind for now, but I will be back within three moons.
 Please do not worry, and do not scry for me.
Watch the shoppe, if you can.
Blessed be, H.

I rolled the scroll, tied it with a black ribbon, and placed it in the middle of the table.

The vampire waited for me by the door.

'Shall we away?' he asked, holding his hand out once more.

I didn't take it, but brushed past him instead. As I stepped over the threshold, Bell jangled softly above me. I looked up at the old bronze bell, faded and scratched with age.

'You have to stay here and watch the shoppe,' I ordered. Bell clanged once in agreement, then stopped immediately as the vampire stroked a long finger along the rim. He met my eyes.

'Very interesting,' he breathed.

Chapter 5

Of course, the vampire prince would have an elaborately decorated carriage!

He may not dress extravagantly, but he obviously wanted the whole world to know who he was.

The carriage was parked on the cobbled street, not far from my door. It was led by four horses with shimmering black coats, and manes that had been braided up with gold ribbons. The whole thing looked like something out of a fairy tale. Well, maybe a nightmare. The carriage was cast in black iron and decorated with gold filigree, with huge wheels that were taller than me.

It looked a lot like a hearse, to be honest – which may have been the whole point, what with him being a vampire prince. A few early morning shoppers began to gather and stop to stare.

I overheard a young couple ask another bystander if there was a film being made. They took out their smartphones and filmed as one of the two drivers climbed down a ladder and unlocked the carriage compartment.

'What's this, H?' Cole asked, appearing suddenly from amidst the growing crowd, rubbing his hands together and stomping his feet to chase away the cold. 'This is pretty,' he added, nodding towards the carriage. 'Is it yours?' he joked.

I scoffed. 'Does it look like something I would go around in?'

'Well,' he began, with a wink. 'It does look fit for a princess.'

I was keenly aware of Heston listening in on our interaction and I felt my cheeks blush pink, when usually I would just roll my eyes at Cole's playful comments. Hopefully, if the vampire noticed, he would just think they were flushed from the cold.

'Shall we go in?' Cole asked, oblivious. 'I'm in dire need of a hot cuppa.'

I felt Heston approach. Cole, who still hadn't seen him, began reaching for the door to the shoppe.

'Actually, Cole, I'm just off out,' I said, nodding my head awkwardly at the carriage.

'Oh, off out, is it?' he said, looking a bit baffled.

'Are you ready to go, Hodge?' Heston asked, while looking down at Cole with a bemused smile.

'Yes,' I said, awkwardly. 'Let's go.'

LIFE'S A WITCH

'Will you be back tonight?' Cole asked.

'I don't think so,' Heston answered for me. I shot him a death glare and turned to Cole. He was looking more and more confused by the moment, and still had a hold of the shoppe door handle, like he was going in.

'I'm not sure. I will call you when I'm home,' I said, apologetically.

'Okay. Do you need me to pass on any messages?' Cole asked, with a meaningful look. I shook my head.

'Hodge, dear?' Heston prompted. I rolled my eyes for Cole's sake and attempted a light smile. I think it came out all weird, though, because Cole furrowed his brow and looked more confused than ever. I couldn't blame him – it wasn't every day you saw a witch hop into a vampire's horse-drawn hearse.

'See you soon!' I waved to him, as cheerfully as I could muster.

Heston was holding his hand out for me by the open carriage door, but I glared at him and brushed past. Unfortunately, the step up was rather high, and I ended up slipping right into his open arms. He chuckled softly and lifted me inside, before climbing in gracefully after me and taking the seat opposite.

The attendant came and locked the door, before bowing his head at Heston and disappearing back up into the driver's cab.

There was a lot of commotion and cheering from the crowd as we disembarked on the bumpy cobblestones. I nodded at Cole as we drove by. The poor man was still standing by the shoppe door, looking dumbfounded. He half raised his hand and then let it fall back again. Then I could no longer see him as we rumbled past the shops.

The inside of the carriage was exactly as I expected, with red velvet seats, lace curtains and plush, circular cushions. I noticed Heston, sitting opposite with one leg gracefully draped over the other, observing me with a small, secret smile.

'This is all a bit much, really,' I observed. He laughed and leant back in his seat.

'Nothing is ever too much for a prince of the night,' he replied.

'Even a limo would have been better than this,' I said.

The carriage was going at an excruciatingly slow pace, slow enough for me to see the surprised reaction of every pedestrian and motorist that we passed on the way. Heston was staring out through the window, looking every bit the handsome villain. Every now and then, he would wave lazily to passers-by; most were confused, some angry, but many from the magical world were excited and would jump, scream or wave as we went past. Heston sat back and smiled at it all, clearly lapping up all the attention.

LIFE'S A WITCH

I found all this mortifying. But, just when I thought I couldn't feel any more embarrassment, we turned onto the dual carriageway.

I let out a loud groan as I covered my face and sunk down into the soft seat so that no one could see me.

'Is this legal?' I asked from behind my fingers. 'You are going to cause an accident.'

'The human police may stop us,' he said casually. 'But the longest I have ever been held is twenty-four hours.'

'What?' I squawked. 'Held? Like, at a police station? I really don't want that.'

'Oh, very well,' he said, as though I was being dramatic. 'I cannot listen to your silly comments the entire journey.' He lifted his arm and rapped on the wall behind his head.

The effect was immediate.

The carriage began to warp oddly, with Heston suddenly seeming to zoom out away from me. My entire body lurched forward and I had a feeling that I must look just as strange. My stomach churned a little bit as the movement suddenly stopped, just as quickly as it had started, like an elastic band being pulled as far as it could, before being quickly let go again.

I pushed my head through the open window to get some air. I was met by the attendant, who had come to open the door. He held his hand out, looking a little sympathetic, and I climbed back down onto solid ground.

We must have travelled magically, because I found myself standing in a gothic courtyard. It was bustling with people and carriages and shiny cars. And, at the centre, was a water fountain made from solid black stone, marbled through with gold.

'Welcome to the Manor,' Heston said, as he descended the carriage behind me.

It didn't look like a manor to me. It looked like a full-blown medieval vampire castle, complete with towers, turrets and scary-looking gargoyles. I had to lean back to see all the way to the top.

'Shall we?' Heston asked, holding his hand out, signalling for me to lead the way. I shook my head a little, not wanting to take the lead and walk through those haughty doors first. Heston shrugged and strolled up the thick stone steps into the castle and I followed awkwardly.

The entrance hall of the Manor, and the corridors beyond, were surprisingly austere looking. There were a lot of attendants in uniform who all bowed to Heston as we walked past. The walls themselves were made from blocks of cream-coloured stone, while the few hanging tapestries that decorated those walls depicted mild seasonal landscapes. I had expected something a bit more... wild, from the home of a vampire king.

'So, how does this work then?' Heston asked suddenly, as we began a fast pace down another corridor. 'The potion?'

'Oh,' I said. 'It's pretty simple.'

LIFE'S A WITCH

'Go on.'

'Well, you just add your saliva to the drink, before you serve it.'

'Saliva? That is disgusting,' he said with a cackle. 'So she just needs to spit in it? That isn't very elegant. I thought it would be something like a lock of hair, or a drop of blood. Will blood do?'

'No, it has to be saliva. I suppose you don't actually have to spit in it, though. You could lick it. It has to be you, though, not the recipient.'

'The potion is not for me, dear witch,' he said. 'It's for my father, so *I* definitely won't be spitting in it.'

'You're trying to spell someone to fall in love with your father?' I said in surprise.

Heston sighed and came to a stop, turning to me and placing his hands on my shoulders. He looked down at me with frustration.

'Please try to keep up, witch. I thought you were smart?'

'Why on earth did you think that?' I asked.

'The spell is for my father to take. I need him to fall in love.' The vampire ignored my last words.

'That sounds a bit twisted,' I said. 'Your father is the king, isn't he? Doesn't he rule over all the vampires, like… everywhere? It seems kind of irresponsible to spell him.'

Heston threw back his head and laughed. When he looked at me again there was a dark glint in his eye.

'Oh, you have no idea, witch,' he said. 'But he has announced his intent to die, and that means I need to act fast.'

'His intent to die?'

'Yes. My father is old, older than any other vampire king in recorded history. I knew it was coming, but I thought I had more time.'

'Is your father dying?' I asked, confused by his wording. Heston looked down at me gently, like I was some very stupid thing that needed his pity.

'Vampires cannot die of old age. We are either disposed of, or we decide to die. My father has decided it is time for him to pass on. And, despite his age, he has only one heir. Me.'

He looked a me then, as though I should completely understand the situation. I looked back, blankly. He shook his head and pushed me forward, continuing his fast-paced walk.

We approached a grand entranceway, with two guards either side, dressed in neat red and black uniforms. They bowed low and pushed open the large, wooden double doors.

'Are you ready?' Heston asked.

'Ready for what?'

Chapter 6

Almost as soon as we walked through into the dazzling ballroom beyond, a female vampire intercepted us. She was tall and beautiful, with sharp features and a mess of blonde curls bundled atop her head. She wore a skin-tight black gown and red gemstones dripped from her neck and ears. I suddenly felt very underdressed and self-conscious in my dusty, patchwork dress. It was clear to me that we had just walked into some kind of grand celebration, already in full swing.

An ocean of couples were dancing around in synchronised circles on the marble floor and a string orchestra was playing a haunting ballad. I craned my neck to get a better view. At the far end of the room, upon a dais, seated on a throne that was completely wrapped in vines of pure black roses, with elongated thorns that stuck out threateningly, was the vampire king. He wore an embroidered black robe that trailed down the steps of the dais. His features were very similar to Heston's. If I didn't know better, I would think them twins, except the king's hair was a light shade of grey. Squinting to see more clearly, I noticed his eyes were black or grey. Definitely not the bright ruby red of Heston's.

'Is that your father…?' I turned back to Heston, just in time to see him whispering urgently to the female vampire. She bowed and disappeared quickly.

'Who was that?' I asked as he grabbed my arm and led me further into the ballroom. The couples parted for us automatically. They nodded or bowed their heads effortlessly at Heston; a few people reached out to brush his clothes, or said his name reverently.

'Heston…' A man dressed in purple robes appeared before us, almost out of thin air. The large, wooden staff in his hands marked him as a wizard. 'You are late,' he said sternly.

He had dark skin that was wrinkled deeply with age. His hair was as white as snow and it trailed down to his feet in a silky sheet, and he had a long beard to match. As I took him in, I couldn't help but wonder how difficult all that would be to brush. He looked like he'd stepped straight out of a storybook.

Heston smiled warmly at him, but his eyes looked dark.

'A vampire is never late, Frank,' he said. 'He arrives when he plans to arrive.'

The wizard looked at him as a parent might look at a misbehaving child, and I sensed that a scolding was incoming.

'What shampoo do you use?' I asked, in an attempt to defuse the situation.

They both turned to me and I felt my face flush a little under their scrutiny. Heston already thought I was slow, and now this very intimidating wizard was sizing me up, no doubt finding me wanting.

'Your hair is very nice,' I continued, simply.

Silence.

'It's my own spell,' answered the wizard, finally. 'The shampoo. I make it myself.'

I opened my mouth to ask for the recipe, but the wizard turned away and walked up to the dais. I stared at the back of his silky white hair as it glided gracefully away.

'That was painful,' said Heston. I nodded silently in agreement.

'Dance with me, won't you?' he asked, holding his hand out for me to take. 'Then no one else will approach us and force you into another awkward exchange.'

I nodded again and held my hand out. Heston pulled me gently into his arms and spun me around so fast that the world flashed by in a blur of red and black. I felt light as Heston guided me around the room, merging with the other dancers effortlessly. I looked straight forward at his chest, as the spinning began to make me feel a little dizzy. He let go of my hand and, with one finger under my chin, lifted my face so that I was looking into his red eyes. He stared down at me silently, and I felt my heart race uncomfortably.

'Why are you spelling your father?' I asked, desperate to fill the silence, but genuinely curious about the answer.

'I need him to have a new heir, before it's too late,' he said. His step didn't faulter when my feet tripped.

He wanted his father to have another child? He wanted his father to conceive a child while under the influence of a love spell? My stomach lurched uncomfortably and I pulled away from Heston's grip. The dancers around us continued their sway.

'I hadn't even considered that,' I admitted.

'Ah, so you aren't heartless, just irresponsible,' he said. 'Who sells two love potions without even considering the consequences?'

'Why would he need a new heir?' I asked. 'He has you.' Heston looked down at me again as though I was very pitiable.

'I do not want to be king,' he said. 'I have tried everything to convince him. I have looked in every rule book, and there is no other option than this. At least, no other option that I am willing to take.'

'Are you joking?' I exclaimed. 'There are so many other options! You could abdicate, or *you* could have a child, or...'

LIFE'S A WITCH

'I am his heir. As such, I am bound to be king. I have no choice. However, if I can convince him to live longer, convince him to crown another in my place…' He hesitated. 'A vampire king cannot abdicate. Once the crown is on your head, a ruler is a ruler until death.'

I couldn't think of anything to say, but just then the music stopped and the dancers ceased their movement, clapping in appreciation of the musicians. Heston and I joined in the clapping, and he took my arm again, once more leading me closer to the dais.

'It just seems like you are being a bit hasty,' I whispered to him. He held a finger up to his lips, ignoring me.

'I feel like there are still so many options,' I continued.

'Shh!' he hissed, tapping his finger to his lips in annoyance. 'It's happening.' He nodded towards the throne of roses and thorns.

'Wait… *it's* happening, like, right now?' I asked.

'No time like the present,' Heston said. 'Will it work right away?'

'It should do,' I said, uncertainly.

I followed his gaze, to see that the blonde vampire from earlier was walking up the dais. She had a large, silver goblet in her hand, and I realised that Heston must have passed it to her at the entrance to the ballroom, while I was looking around.

The pretty vampire bowed down low to the floor as she approached the king, and handed the potion up to him.

The king took it from her thankfully and waved for her to stand. She did so, while catching Heston's eye and winking conspiratorially at him.

'Wow,' I said, suddenly feeling very anxious as I watched the king down the potion from his goblet.

I took an involuntary step backwards as he greedily shook the last dregs into his open mouth.

'I really wish you hadn't told me your plan!' I hissed in a panic. 'This is getting a little bit too non-consenty, and a bit gross, so I think I'm going to go.' I stepped back again.

'You didn't care about how gross it was when you gave that grandma a potion for me,' replied Heston.

'Uh, true, but two wrongs don't make a right.'

'I'm a vampire, a prince of darkness and decay. I don't care about wrong or right. I just do not want to be king.'

'Well, that's neither here nor there,' I mumbled as I stepped back yet again, trying to subtly make my way to the doors behind us. 'Besides,' I admonished, 'you are way closer to that grandma's age than you are to half the women you date publicly!'

'Stop worrying so much,' he scolded. 'I'm not as despicable as you think. She is a trustworthy woman and has promised to not…uh, take advantage of my father until the spell has worn off. She is to marry him and become pregnant. The child doesn't have to be his biological son.'

'This all seems really confusing to me,' I said. 'Couldn't he just adopt if his heir doesn't have to be blood related?'

LIFE'S A WITCH

However, Heston didn't reply to my questions. He was too busy staring, in complete horror, at the vampire king, who was suddenly, very clearly, choking.

The king stood up from his throne, clutching at his throat in panic. A few women slapped him hard on his back and cried out for help. Heston ran over to his father, just before the king collapsed to the floor. He blinked up at his son in shock for a few moments, and then was still.

I stepped back quickly into the surging crowd and made a run for the doors. But Heston's voice boomed over the horrified silence of the ballroom.

'Don't let her leave!' he bellowed.

The guards nearest raced over and slammed the large marble doors shut in my face, trapping me in.

Well, shit.

Chapter 7

'So, this is awkward,' I said with a nervous laugh.

Heston stared at me from the throne of thorns, looking very unamused, his father's crown crooked on his head, exactly how the minister had placed it a few hours ago. It was carved from bone and adorned with large black gemstones that engulfed any light that dared to touch it.

'It's not "awkward", witch!' he said, mimicking my voice. 'It's a bloody disaster!'

'Well, how was I to know that would happen?' I snapped back. 'I didn't mean to kill him. You're the one that gave him the cursed potion.'

'What an amazing witch you are,' he replied. 'You have singlehandedly managed to give me the exact opposite of everything I asked for.'

LIFE'S A WITCH

'Well, I wouldn't say it was singlehandedly. You had a pretty decent-sized hand in it, too!'

'I have one question, witch, and don't you dare try to lie to me,' said the vampire, his face serious. 'Did you poison that potion purposefully, to kill me?'

'No!' I cried, appalled that he thought I would do such a thing.

'Did you make it with the intention of killing or harming any person who would drink it?'

'No,' I said again, firmly. 'I am almost certain that it wasn't my potion that caused this. It must have been tampered with.'

The vampire slammed his fist into the throne in anger, and then yelped instantly in pain.

'Why would you make a throne out of thorns?' He said. 'This is the most uncomfortable, stupid…'

He stood up and pointed at a random attendant.

'You! Bring me a better chair, one with velvet and gold, and a cupholder.'

'I'm not sure how intimidating that is going to look…' I mumbled under my breath.

'Hmm? What's that, witch?' he shouted angrily. 'You want to make remarks? Well, that's perfect, because if I am to be stuck here, then so too shall you be.' Dread welled up inside of me. 'That's right.' The vampire smiled, seeing the panic on my face. 'You, witch, are going to be…' He looked around as if for inspiration. 'The new Royal wizard!'

He turned to the old wizard who had remained standing behind the throne all this time, not moving, even when the king's body was removed. He looked very pale and seemed to be swaying slightly in shock.

'Sorry, Frank,' Heston said dismissively, before gesturing to the attendants. 'Take Frank to the oubliette!' he commanded. An attendant hurried up to Heston and bowed so low that his head almost hit the floor. When he popped up again, he whispered something into Heston's ear. Heston groaned dramatically and rolled his eyes. '*Build* an oubliette, and *then* put Frank in there,' he snapped. 'Just take him away!'

There was a slight scuffle as the wizard Frank was led away by a group of very reluctant, and slightly confused, guards. It seemed to last a long time, as the wizard was swaying oddly. I stood mortified, trying very hard to not make eye contact with the white-haired mage, who I could feel was glaring daggers at me.

'Don't be too glum,' Heston said once the large wooden doors had finally closed behind them. 'He was an awful person.' I looked up at him, suspiciously. 'Well, he was probably awful,' he went on. 'You don't get to be the Royal wizard in a vampire palace by being jolly and friendly, do you?'

'Heston,' I growled.

'*King* Heston,' he corrected.

'I am not going to be your wizard,' I said firmly.

LIFE'S A WITCH

Heston smiled at me then, flashing the tips of his fangs. He stepped down from the dais and made his way over to me. We were alone in the large ballroom now, as all the attendants were either looking for a chair to satisfy the king's requirements, or building an oubliette for the Royal warlock.

I stood my ground as the vampire stopped in front of me. Gently, he took my chin in his elegant, be-ringed hand and pulled my face up so that I had no option but to look right into his blood-red eyes. I couldn't help but grimace. Clearly, this was his preferred way of trying to assert his dominance.

'I know, dear witch, that it is easy to forget who and what I am. But, trust me when I say, that refusing me is not in your power.'

I wanted to argue, but my throat dried up and I couldn't find my voice. It struck me again how beautiful and terrifying he was. He smirked, as though he knew exactly what I was thinking. Then he leant in, so that his mouth hovered only inches from mine and I could feel his warm breath.

'Don't fall in love with me, Hodge,' he whispered. My face flushed angrily and I pushed away from the vampire with all my might.

'That is not something you need to worry about,' I insisted, embarrassed. He chuckled. The sound was low and seductive, but I wasn't about to let myself get worked up over a fuckwit, good-for-nothing, egotistical vampire king.

Heston clicked his tongue in disproval. 'So many names, it sounds like you are already worked up,' he said, as he walked back to the dais.

My face flushed even brighter. I could feel my cheeks burning and prickling in embarrassment. How long had he been able to read my mind? The entire time? I was going to whip up a spell to shut him out, as soon as I was able.

Attendants began flooding into the room, carrying an armchair. It was plated with gold and upholstered in purple velvet.

'Majesty, we could not find a chair matching your exact needs,' said one attendant. 'However, the Royal carpenters are crafting you a throne now, and it will be ready by tomorrow.' The attendant bowed low, clumsily dropping his end of the chair. Heston waved his hand at him, as though he was an annoyance.

'Exactly which features are not to my specification?' he asked.

'We could not find one with a cupholder, oh Darkest One,' the attendant lamented. Heston tsked in annoyance.

'That was the most important part,' he sighed. 'Oh, very well, it will have to do for now. One of you will be my Royal cupholder.' I rolled my eyes. This man was infuriating.

The attendants placed down the chair and Heston sat in it.

'Fetch me a drink,' he ordered. For a moment, no one moved, unsure who he was talking to. Then the attendant who had dropped the chair earlier took it upon himself to be the Royal drink bringer and raced off.

'I can't be a Royal wizard,' I argued again, trying to bring the conversation back on track.

'You can be anything I declare you to be, that's the beauty of being king,' Heston said. 'I make difficult, nonsensical and mostly impossible demands, and all the little ants around me scurry to grant them.'

'Sounds like you will make a great king,' I muttered.

'I never claimed I would be a great king,' he replied. 'I never wanted to *be* king, remember, dear witch? It's you that has landed us in this mess.'

'You know, you could *try* to be a great king. If you hated your father so much, why don't you change things?'

'We old vampires are stuck in our ways,' replied Heston. 'We don't much like change.'

'Well, you just changed a thousand-year-old throne, and threw out a wizard who looked older than this palace.'

'True, I guess I am a man of contradictions,' he smirked.

He was infuriating!

'You may leave me now,' he continued. 'I presume the council will be here to fight over my regard soon, and I am sure you want to settle in.'

'Settle in where?' I asked hesitantly.

'The Royal wizard lives in the alchemist tower,' replied Heston. 'You will like it, I think.' I opened my mouth to protest, but Heston waved a hand irritably. 'Attendant, take my new Royal wizard— No.' He stopped and looked at me, his eyes glowing playfully, and the corners of his mouth turned up in a smirk. 'My dear Royal *witch*, to the alchemist tower, and see she gets some new robes. In forest green, to match her eyes.'

Damn him.

Chapter 8

The tower was beautiful. However, the poor attendant had almost died walking me up there. He had been one of the men carrying the chair, and seemed very happy to be given a new task.

He was already looking a bit frazzled and worn out by the time he got me to the base of the tower. He looked at me, with a manic expression, as he informed me that there were over a thousand steps up to the top.

A few times he had needed to stop, and, to save grace, pretended to show me something interesting in the stonework, a famous signature scratched in, or a rare bug nesting between the mortar. I could see nothing but plain, grey brick. However, I nodded and feigned interest every time he paused. He was only young, and probably quite handsome on any other day. His hair was flaming red, almost as bright as Heston's eyes.

When we reached the top, a marble phoenix stood in our way. It held a glowing blue gemstone in its talons.

'Touch the stone, Royal witch,' gasped the exhausted attendant.

I hesitated, but placed my fingertips on the blue stone. It tingled a little, and the stone flashed brighter and brighter until it was almost blinding and I had to shield my eyes. Then, it very suddenly dulled back to a warm glow, at which point it had morphed into a large, square-cut emerald.

'That's a bit magic,' said the attendant in awe.

'Didn't you know that was going to happen?' I asked, alarmed.

'Oh, no. I figured it would either let you in, or kill you.'

I immediately regretted being so kind to him.

The marble phoenix turned of its own accord, revealing the room beyond. It was a large, circular glass dome. The view was breath-taking. The moon was huge in the sky, lighting up the piles and shelves of books and potions. There was a four-poster bed, a sunken bath, a large kitchenette with a brickwork fireplace, and the biggest cauldron I had ever seen. In the middle of the room was a large, rounded table, with scrolls, thick, dusty tomes, and trays of dubious-looking contents scattered haphazardly all over it.

There was also a small plate with a half-eaten slice of bread, a pat of butter and a cold cup of tea. I felt guilty. This had been the wizard's home. He had expected to come back to it. All his life's work was here, clearly visible. I felt as though I was intruding.

'It's a little messy,' said the attendant. He shuffled around, stacking papers and picking up rubbish. When he got to the plate, I stopped him.

'No, leave it. I will do it,' I said awkwardly. The idea of moving the wizard's stuff made me feel a little queasy. Like, maybe he would come back, and be mad that someone threw out the rest of his food.

'Suit yourself,' said the attendant. He shrugged and placed the papers back. 'I will get some attendants in to change the bedding,' he added.

I thanked him, but had already decided I didn't want to sleep on the bed. There was a window seat in an alcove that had cushions scattered on it, that looked just big enough for me to curl up on.

'If you want, I could be your personal attendant,' said the man.

'And risk walking up those stairs several times a day?' I laughed. 'I'm not sure I could do that to you.'

He looked at me unconvinced.

'Really? I think it's much better than ending up as the Royal pillow fluffer, or arse wiper.' He rolled his eyes to the ceiling.

I liked this guy.

'Fine, it makes no odds to me,' I replied. 'But, be warned, I am going to be the worst Royal wizard there ever was. I need to get this vampire off my back.'

The attendant looked thoughtful for a moment.

'That would be a challenge, since there was once a Royal wizard who was literally a pig. I will do my best to help, though.'

'A pig… why? Wait. What did you say?'

'Well, it was all down to Princess Greta. She was only seven when she became queen, bless her. It didn't last long, but the bacon was—'

'No, not the pig,' I said. 'You said you would help?'

'Why not? Nothing else to do,' he said, shrugging. 'It all depends on whether you want to be incompetent, or downright dangerous. I'm up for either – or both, of course.'

I was starting to feel like this attendant was a bit of a wild card. He paced around the large table, inspecting the papers and nibbling on the wizard's bread.

'We'd call this slice a doorstop where I come from. You want a bite?' he asked, misunderstanding my look.

'What's your name?' I asked, ignoring the question.

'Call me Finn,' he replied, his mouth full of what must have been very stale bread.

'Is Finn your real name?' I asked. He smiled conspiratorially in response.

'I'm a fairy, so I think I will keep my real name to myself,' Finn responded.

LIFE'S A WITCH

That was fair. I knew that, in fairy lore, names had power. I decided I wouldn't hand mine over easily, either.

I took another look around the wizard's room, taking in the complete chaos of the wizard's possessions, and sighed. No matter what, I would probably have to stay here for a little while. I couldn't leave it like this.

'Finn, I've changed my mind. Can you clear this room? Make sure you keep all the paperwork and notes, though.'

'The guilt didn't last long, then?' Finn said, laughing heartily. He pushed the rest of the bread into his mouth, then downed the last dregs of what must be stone-cold tea. He didn't stop there, though, as he promptly ate the mug and plate. The crunching, slurping noises rooted me to the spot in some kind of curious horror for a few moments. Then I made a hasty retreat back to the stone phoenix, keeping my eyes on the hungry fairy the whole time.

As I made my way back down the tower stairs, I noticed that the walls were covered in shimmering signatures and hastily scribbled notes. There were recipes, love letters and spells. There were plenty of colourful, long-legged bugs, too…

I needed to get out of this odd place.

Chapter 9

Bizarre.

Completely bizarre.

The Manor was enchanted. No doubt about it.

Things that had looked very normal, boringly so, on the way in, were suddenly upside down and topsy-turvy.

The walls, which before were made of grey stone and mortar, were now multicoloured, glowing and shimmering in dark purple and orange hues, and the walls themselves seemed to be pulsing. It was making me feel slightly seasick. An oil painting depicting shady-looking characters moved – not just the subjects, but the canvas itself spun and shifted.

Vampires, dressed in finery, strolled arm in arm with goblins, pixies, trolls and even witches.

I had an odd feeling that maybe the castle had always looked this way. Perhaps the act of touching the phoenix stone, or walking into the wizard's tower, had stripped away the glamour.

Or maybe it had cursed me?

My fellow witches nodded in recognition as they passed me, and I back at them, but no words were exchanged between us.

The palace was bustling with loud chamber music that seemed to seep from the very walls. It kept to an even tone as I walked down hallway after hallway.

Attendants ran here, there and everywhere, carrying silver trays loaded with drinks, pastries, or even entire animal carcasses. They were beginning to seem like the most normal thing about this place, because I found myself feeling a sense of relief every time I saw one.

Sometimes, the corridors twisted and turned, or shrank so small that I was sure I was heading for a dead end and would be trapped. However, there was always a frantic attendant running ahead of me and opening some secret door or another, indirectly showing me the way.

Mostly, the halls were lit with braziers, or fireplaces, but sometimes they were illuminated by thousands of enchanted black candles that floated along the ceilings, casting disturbing shadows on the walls and drawing attention to the ribbons of cobwebs that decorated every corner, tapestry, painting and fixture.

When I found myself in a room filled with nothing but intricately decorated coffins, of all shapes and sizes, I realised

I could take no more. I grabbed hold of the next attendant I saw – a small, human-looking woman with bright pink hair that was tied into buns. She was carrying two trays of tall martini glasses that were filled with a steaming red liquid. I could only hope it wasn't blood.

'I am so lost, can you show me the way to the throne room, please?' I asked her desperately.

'Just ask the door, silly.' She nodded her head to the door I had just passed through, before placing the trays down near a large, black coffin.

I cried out as the coffin flipped open and a slim, grey hand shot out, grabbing one of the glasses and disappearing again. The attendant looked at me as though I was the insane one.

'Please don't wake the Masters,' she scolded, before turning back and out the door again.

I followed and paused at the door she had told me to ask. At this point, I could believe anything.

'Uh… Door?' I ventured awkwardly. 'Could you open up onto the throne room?' I hesitated, before adding, 'Please?' I felt unbelievably stupid as I took hold of the handle and pulled the door open. I think I would have been slightly disappointed if I hadn't seen the glittering throne room beyond. I felt a weird sort of pride swell in my chest when it was there. 'Thank you,' I said earnestly, before stepping from the dark coffin room into the opulent ballroom.

I immediately regretted my decision, though, as it was clear I was walking into some kind of fight, already in motion. A man, covered in purple bruises, was being dragged along the floor in front of me by two attendants, while another, who was clearly the assailant, watched. He proudly thumped his fists on his bare chest.

I spun around to walk back through the door, only to find it had disappeared. Instead, I was staring at hundreds of faces, all standing behind a thick, velvet rope.

The crowds of people pushed against the rope, jeering, laughing and pointing at me.

Not ideal.

They all seemed to be very interested in watching me, and some were gesturing wildly and trying to talk to me. I couldn't make out any individual words, however, as the noise was too loud.

I was pretty sure they were heckling me.

Suddenly, I recognised Finn's face in the crowd. He jostled to the front and shook his head at me, looking more than slightly embarrassed. He was mouthing and pointing emphatically to something behind me.

I turned around.

Shit.

The fighter from before had been replaced by a beast of a man who was currently charging toward me at full speed.

He looked to be at least part troll. I had a split second to take in his grey skin, black eyes, wild green hair and bulging muscles before he slammed into me, knocking me off my feet. I hit the deck and landed hard on my back, completely winded.

I lay for a few moments, stunned, trying to gasp for air. Finn appeared by my side and pulled me into a sitting position.

'Come on, now, just calm down and take a big ol' breath,' he said, sounding more exasperated than concerned.

'What the hell was that?' I rasped when I could finally get a grip.

'That is Grant, and I suggest you get up and face him before the gong rings and you become a witch-shaped pancake.'

'What?' But Finn was already pulling me up onto my feet. He thumped my aching back encouragingly and pushed me forward into the middle of what, I was beginning to realise, was some kind of entertainment ring. Opposite me stood Grant, his shoulders heaving as he breathed, his eyes glaring into my soul and baying for my blood.

'Uh, no thanks,' I said, backing up until I came into contact with the velvet rope behind me.

'Too late for that!' cried a few people from the crowd. They laughed heartily. Some of them were eating popcorn, or drinking from elaborately shaped cocktail glasses.

A bell rang out, signalling the next round, and Grant wasted no time in charging. He let out a loud roar and I thought I would die right then and there. Instead, I shut my eyes and hurriedly reached out for my magic. I felt the crackle of it in the air and hurriedly set up a shielding spell, cursing under my breath the entire time.

The crush of Grant's body colliding with the invisible spell was a sound I wouldn't forget in a hurry. The room erupted in noise; some people cheered, others swore and threw their food in my general direction. A very soggy bun landed directly on top of my head. I shook it off.

Grant didn't stay down for long. He snorted loudly at me, and I was sure I saw steam blow out from his large nostrils.

Well, that was enough for me.

I tried to hop back over the velvet rope, but the crowds of people pushed against me, jeering and booing.

'What are you doing?' Finn hissed, suddenly at my side. 'Are you the Royal witch or aren't you? Get back out there! Don't embarrass me.'

Embarrass him? I was about to be flattened by a giant half-man half-beast. I didn't care about embarrassing a crockery-eating attendant. How did I even get here?! That cursed door had a whole lot to answer for!

'I don't know how to fight,' I complained.

'Just use magic,' said Finn. 'The only rule is to wait for the gong. After that, it's fair game!' As if on cue, the gong rang out again. Finn hurried backed away to the safe zone.

'Oh, sure! Let him back over!' I yelled.

Finn was right, though. I was a witch. I may not have brawn, and I may not have brains… but I certainly had… well, I'm not sure what I had, but I would try my best.

SIMONE NATALIE

I dashed out of the way as Grant raced towards me. He didn't seem to have much steering ability, because it took him a few seconds to stop and change course. I easily evaded him again, waiting until the moment before impact and stepping just out of his way. A few people laughed and cheered at this. Maybe I was gaining some fans?

Grant, roaring in frustration, whipped out one of his large hands and grabbed my upper arm. I tried to pull free, but his grip was like a vice. My whole arm ached from it.

'Let me go!' I demanded, stupidly. He threw back his head and laughed as I tried to pry open his chunky fingers. Effortlessly, he lifted me off the floor and waved me around.

This was really starting to hurt now.

I lifted my free hand and chanted words of power under my breath. Blue flames erupted around my closed fist. I quickly slammed it, with as much force as I could, into the side of Grant's face. My punch alone wouldn't have made any impact, but the fire quickly took a hold of his hair and began to spread. He yelped and dropped me to the floor. I landed badly on my ankle and yelped as the pain shot up my leg.

'What is going on here!' boomed a familiar voice. 'I was gone for ten minutes and you are already trying to assassinate my Royal wizard?'

'My Lord, she volunteered!' someone cried from the crowd.

LIFE'S A WITCH

'I highly doubt that.' Heston stepped over the ring, grabbing a glass from a spectator as he passed by. He threw the contents of the glass at Grant's hair and the fire went out with an angry hiss.

'Hmm, you're lucky. I thought that was alcohol,' he mused as Grant bowed thankfully. 'What are the odds?' Heston laughed.

Grant smiled sheepishly, unsure if the king was joking or not.

Heston dropped the glass and crouched on the ground next to me, a bemused look on his face.

'What are you playing at?' he chuckled. I opened my mouth to retort, but pain shot up my leg and I faltered.

'You're hurt,' he stated and, before I could answer, he lifted me up in his arms. It hurt a little, but he pulled me close to his chest. I expected every step to be agony, but he walked like a ghost, gliding along the floor effortlessly. People around us stared openly as they parted and bowed for their king. More than one person glared daggers at me, nestled in Heston's arms.

'Can you put me down, please?' I asked, embarrassed by the whole situation.

I felt his low chuckle rumble in his chest.

'Do you really want that?' he asked, looking down at me as if I was a broken lamb, and not a powerful witch. 'I don't think you can walk right now.'

'I don't need to walk. I could just fly,' I retorted. I shuffled and tried to hop out of his arms, biting down on my lips to stop from gasping from the pain.

'I'm taking you to the infirmary, then you can do whatever you like,' he said, all humour gone.

'I don't need the infirmary, I just need to make a healing potion,' I insisted.

'You want to attempt to walk up to the tower?' he asked. 'Or do you want me to carry you up there?' His mouth curved into a wide smirk. How I hated that smirk. He looked at me then, and slowly leant down until his lips brushed softly against my ear. 'Do you hate it, little witch? Really?' he breathed. I felt goosebumps erupt over my skin and I forcefully pushed him away.

He snickered again.

'We're here, anyway,' he said as he gently laid me down on a small, single bed. I looked around at what appeared to be a large hospital ward, with dozens of beds all made up neatly with simple white linens. Bright blue partitions separated them all, blocking the view of some that must have been already occupied.

A tall vampire with thick black hair rushed over. She wore a pure white lab coat, and was exactly like the kind of doctor you would see on TV – perfect and glossy. She held a large clipboard in her hands, had a pocket full of pens, and a stethoscope hanging around her shoulders. She bowed low to Heston and, for a moment, I felt a little stunned by her beauty. She had black skin that shimmered like silk, irises of pure, sparkling gold and cheekbones as sharp as a knife. Her beauty wasn't dark and inhuman like Heston's; it was breathtaking.

'How can I help?' she asked.

'I think my witch has broken her foot,' Heston said, seemingly unfazed by the beauty before him.

'Then I will run some tests, and order an X-ray, oh Darkest One,' she replied, while taking notes.

Just then, Finn appeared at Heston's side, looking very frantic. He bowed hastily to Heston, then glared at me. Under the pretence of comforting me, he leant in to pat my back and hissed in my ear.

'You forfeited the match. I had three gold coins down for you to win!'

Rude.

'Are you a witch, or aren't you?' he said.

'I'm really more of a potion witch,' I explained. 'I've never been great at spell casting, that is more Morga—' I cut off quickly, realising I was about to talk about my family. I didn't want anyone here knowing about Morgan, Raven or Granny.

Finn rolled his eyes. He then opened his mouth, no doubt to scold me again, but suddenly he was yanked up out of my eyeline, his small feet dangling in the air where his head had been seconds before. Heston had grabbed him up by his silk collar and lifted him, almost to the ceiling.

Finn bowed his head down to his chin, as Heston shook him lazily.

'Your job is to look after *my* witch, attendant. Yet, she has been hurt on your watch. How shall I punish you?' Finn squirmed and apologised profusely for his failing.

'It's not his fault,' I protested. 'If you should punish anyone, it would be that damned door. I was so polite to it, too,' I complained.

Heston dropped the fairy and turned his full gaze to me. 'The door?' he asked.

'Yeah, I was lost, so I asked the door to take me to the throne room. But it dropped me off right in the middle of that ring!'

Heston seemed to consider this a moment, his face blank, a mask of beauty that looked like it could have been carved from marble. It almost hurt to stare for too long.

'What was it doing there, anyway?' I asked Finn, anxious to look away from the vampire. 'The ring?'

'The games have begun, of course,' he answered jovially, as he readjusted himself, plumping up his cravat and brushing down his clothes. 'The late king's funeral will be held in seven days, under the new blood moon.'

'And you mourn by playing games?' I asked, confused.

'No, it's not that kind of game,' he said. 'A long time ago, before the games, the time of mourning was utter chaos, as the staff of the old ruler would be replaced by the new ruler's favourites. There was a lot of backstabbing. And, I mean that literally – people were getting stabbed. It was pretty bleak.

'So, one of the old Royal wizards came up with the games as a chance for any member of the Manor to show off their skills and prove themselves worthy of the job. The winner is guaranteed their preferred spot, and everyone is too distracted to kill each other.'

'It's an honour,' the vampire doctor interjected. 'I am hoping to win the knife throw myself,' she added enthusiastically. 'I am *very* good with a scalpel.' The way she said this sent an unpleasant chill down my back, but Heston and Finn both looked suitably impressed.

'Best of luck to you, I say,' said Heston. The vampire doctor smiled and bowed low.

'I will win in your name, my Lord,' she continued. 'To earn a spot as your Royal physician.'

Heston nodded encouragingly. I wondered, then, if the current Royal physician would shortly be heading for the newly built oubliette, as well…

'After the mourning period, the celebration of our wicked king's coronation will begin!' Finn announced, bowing low. I couldn't tell if he was truly as excited by the prospect of all this celebrating, or if he was trying to suck up to the king, in the hope of not ending up in the oubliette himself.

'Yes, and that has reminded me, that I must go,' said Heston, his face darkening. 'My dear uncle is blessing us with a visit and I have much to prepare.'

SIMONE NATALIE

    Finn met my eye and mouthed, 'Oh dear.'
    Heston gave a withering look, then shot one more nod at the doctor. With that, he strolled away, leaving me wondering how *dear* this uncle really was to him.

Chapter 10

The vampiric doctor turned out to be a pretty normal, and very chatty, doctor. She took my bloods, sent me for scans and checked my vitals. When she was happy with everything, she offered me a tailor-made potion to heal the fracture. It looked very similar to one of my own, actually.

She explained, when I asked, that most medicine used in the castle was human made. However, when it came to some things, magic was just better. They had pharmacists, chemists and alchemists on site at all times.

All in all, I was only on the ward for a few hours before I was cleared.

The doctor, who told me to call her Posy, was in no rush to let me go, however, and invited me over to her rooms for a night for spiced cocktails.

After a bit of coercing, I agreed that I would go after the knife games, to either celebrate her win, or commiserate her loss.

My foot felt better than ever when I left the ward, and I was starting to feel a little bit silly for all the hassle I had caused.

I kept recollecting the way Heston had carried me, pulled close to his body, like I didn't weigh anything, when in reality I was a tall, chubby Broome witch. We weren't built to be carried around; we were bult to *do* the carrying.

We were built to carry our coven, our community and our history. I felt a little pang of guilt, then, thinking about the shoppe and the letter I had left for Raven. Without a doubt, Morgan would have rushed straight to his mother that morning, to tell her what had happened, and the letter would only have worried them more.

Raven would have to watch the shoppe. The burden of it had weighed heavily on me, but it would be harder still on her.

She had been a typical witch all our childhood. However, after her initiation, when her full powers came in, she struggled with control. Raven was a strong conduit for magic, and, as time went on, she became afraid of her strength and what it could do. Granny tried to help her, the coven tried to help her, but her heart wasn't in it; and so, two years after her initiation, she performed a power-binding spell on herself.

LIFE'S A WITCH

It had hit Granny hard at the time.

Raven went to a normal college, got married, then divorced, became a police officer and stayed as far away from magic as she could. That was, until Morgan began to explore the powers of magic a few years ago.

Now, I was forcing her to take care of the shoppe, and her worst fears were coming true – her sister was missing, leaving only her to act as head of the coven.

I had no idea how long I would be stuck in the Manor, but hopefully it wouldn't be too long. Maybe Heston would let me send Raven a letter of reassurance…

I was broken out of my reverie by the very loud sounds of my stomach rumbling.

This seemed to set off the whole corridor! It came alive with sudden bursts of bright green and purple light flaring from ceiling to floor.

The lights flashed and strobed intermittently, causing me to feel a bit ill. I carried on down the excitable hallway until the lights faded a little into a warmer spectrum of colour.

I recognised this part of the Manor. The sound of raised voices confirmed that I had made my way back to the corridor that led to the throne room.

'I don't want to join the games, so could you not?' I said to no one in particular, just in case anyone or anything was listening. I let out a little shriek as a portrait on the wall beside me suddenly emitted a loud 'whooping' noise and spun around as if in answer.

SIMONE NATALIE

I took a chance and leant in closer to look. It was hard to tell with all the spinning, but it looked like an oil painting of a horse and rider. The horse was a little palomino. Its rider, a blonde-haired, pink-eyed vampire, looked far too big for it.

'Excuse me?' I asked the spinning image. 'Can you point me in the direction of the kitchen? Or, even better, a bathroom.' I hadn't asked before, and I couldn't face having to climb up those tower steps every single time I needed the toilet, and I couldn't trust the doors after last time.

The picture whooshed louder and spun faster, obviously showing off now that it had my attention.

A light chuckle behind me caused the hair on the back of my neck to stand on end. I spun around to find the corridor behind me filled with vampires.

At the helm of the extravagantly dressed group was a man. He was more masculine than any vampire I had met so far, with broad shoulders and thick arms, but his eyes were red and he had the familiar aura around him that only vampires seemed to have. It was an odd otherworldliness, as though the air around them didn't know how to react to their presence, as though they weren't supposed to be here.

'The paintings aren't very helpful,' the man said, with a smirk on his face. 'They are barely sentient, really.'

'Oh?' I said, trying to feign interest while I flittered around, looking for an exit. There was something malicious about this man. My magic was escaping and crackling in the air around me, giving off a little warning.

If he noticed, he didn't address it.

'No,' he said, advancing on me. 'My great, great, grandmother was a witch, you know, and she spelled them. Among many other things in this Manor.' The vampire stopped a few feet before me and, very slowly, pulled off the black gloves he had been wearing, revealing pale, thin, bejewelled hands.

'It's good to be home,' he said with a smile. He looked down at me warmly. His face was soft and the slight stubble over his jaw made him look more human, but he was definitely a vampire.

'I can lead you to the nearest guest bathroom,' he continued, holding his arm out for me to take. 'Though, I can see you are no guest here.' A large part of me wanted to ask how he could see that, but alarm bells were still jingling in my head and I had trouble finding my voice.

Softly, he took my hand and placed it in the crook of his arm. 'Shall we?'

I nodded and we walked, arm in arm, for a moment. He led me past the throne room and away from any signs of civilisation. A quick look behind me showed that his entourage had held back and did not come with us. Why was that? I swallowed hard, getting a horrible feeling in the pit of my stomach.

SIMONE NATALIE

The vampire led me through a small black door and down another corridor. This one was lit by the floating candles only, and I could no longer hear chamber music. I dared a sneaky look up at him, but he stared dead ahead. I had the distinct feeling that I was about to be 'disposed of'.

Then, from behind us, came loud, hurried footsteps beating on the wooden floor. I didn't dare turn around, but the footsteps grew quicker and quicker as they approached.

'Uncle!' cried a familiar voice. I felt my shoulders relax and I let out a long sigh of relief as Heston took my arm and pulled me away from the stocky vampire.

'Heston! Dear boy!' cried the older vampire, who I presumed to be Heston's visiting uncle.

Heston looked at me meaningfully, his ruby red eyes flicking over every inch of my face to make sure I was unharmed. When he was satisfied, he placed me behind him and fixed his uncle with a deathly glare.

'What are you doing down here with my Royal witch?' he demanded.

'Uh, is that who she is?' asked the uncle in all innocence. 'Well, the lady was a bit lost, and needed the use of a bathroom,' he explained, lowering his voice.

'I found your friends from the Court of Bone, abandoned in the hallway,' said Heston.

'Ah, yes. Well, the young witch seemed a little rattled, so I thought it would be *indelicate* for us all to escort her,' the uncle explained.

LIFE'S A WITCH

That all sounded fairly reasonable, actually.

Had I been overreacting? But, then again, if he really was just taking me to the bathroom, why were we down here in this dark, narrow little hallway? However, as I looked around, it didn't seem so dark now. It just seemed like a normal corridor. As if to prove the point, an attendant ran past, bowing hastily before disappearing into a room to the left. As the door banged shut, I saw it had a W/C sign hanging from it.

Ah.

'Is this the truth?' Heston asked me, turning his back on his uncle and lowering his voice. 'Is it *only* as he says?'

'Uh, actually, yes it is,' I said, feeling silly. The adrenalin rush was wearing off and it was becoming very clear to me that most of my panic had been in my own head.

'Your magic was going haywire,' Heston said. 'I followed its trail all the way here.'

'I didn't know you could do that!' I said, surprised.

'Me, neither,' he replied with a small smile, as he casually placed a hand on my hip. I visibly shivered at the touch as a zip of static electricity flew between us. I looked up at him, expecting to see his usual mocking smirk, but his face was humourless. He stared down at me with an odd look, one I had never seen before. His mouth was open slightly, his brows furrowed. Was it anger? Could he be mad that I had caused so much hassle over nothing?

Slowly, his other hand rose and, light as a feather, he tucked a wisp of my hair behind my ear.

'I was… very concerned,' he said quietly, so that only I could hear. His eyes searched mine and, not for the first time, I was struck by how beautiful they were. They weren't a blood red, like I had thought before. They were deep, layered, like flames. His gaze flicked down to my lips and his hold on my hip tightened. He looked up slowly, meeting my eyes.

My heart skipped a beat and I pushed away abruptly, horrified.

Heston blinked a couple of times at me, as if he had just come out of a daze. The whole exchange had lasted mere seconds, but it felt like I had been staring at him for an age.

I felt my face burn hot as I remembered his uncle was still here. He was watching our interaction with interest.

Heston seemed to be recollecting the same thing. He pulled back his shoulders and stepped away from me.

'Uncle, you must be tired from the journey.' Heston took a hold of his uncle's arm and began leading the way back up the corridor. I remained rooted to the spot.

'We will throw a celebration tonight, to welcome you home!'

Their voices faded down the corridor as they walked away. Heston didn't look back.

LIFE'S A WITCH

I stood there a long while after they had disappeared into the darkness. My heart was still beating erratically and my face felt flushed.

'Are you in the line?' asked an attendant, pointing to the toilet. I nodded and stepped inside.

I was *not* going to fall for a fuckwit vampire.

Chapter 11

My attendance at the party was mandatory, apparently.

Almost the very moment Finn and I had sat down at my table in the tower to eat some well-deserved chocolate cake with a steaming cup of tea, an attendant had come literally crawling up from the tower steps to announce that I was invited to a party that night. It was a dual celebration of the gladiator games concluding and Uncle Trevor arriving.

'Why do they all have such… bland names?' I asked Finn, as I handed the tired attendant a glass of water and pulled out a chair for him to recover in.

'Well, they are all pretty old,' he replied. 'Maybe their names were popular in their time. Just like how Hedgehog is popular now.' He took a long sip of tea.

'Point taken,' I mumbled.

'So, what are you wearing to this thing?' Finn asked.

LIFE'S A WITCH

'I don't know. What I am wearing now, I suppose?' I said, pointing down at my faded patchwork dress. Finn scrunched his face and shook his head.

'Well, there is nothing else for it,' I said. 'All of my things are at the shoppe, and I doubt Heston is going to let me go back there to get them.'

'No,' said Finn thoughtfully. 'He sent some attendants out this afternoon to get everything, but I suppose they aren't back yet.'

'He what?' The thought of random attendants showing up at my home and riffling through my things made me feel queasy. What if Raven or Morgan where there? What if they broke something, or disturbed my dust?

'Don't worry, they won't be too long,' said Finn. 'For now, though, we need to find you something else.'

'No way,' I said stubbornly. Heston could take me just as I was, with my messy hair and hand-me-down dress. If he wanted to show off his new Royal witch, then he could just think again.

As if on cue, two more attendants appeared at the top of the tower carrying a large black dress-box. I smirked as they placed the box on the ground and opened it, revealing a sparking emerald-green robe, nestled among black paper.

'A…gift… from… His Darkness,' panted one of the attendants.

'Well, why didn't he just send all three of you at the same time?' Finn asked as he gathered up the box.

'He did,' said the first attendant, who was recovering with a cup of tea. 'They were slower.'

'And you didn't think to help them?' I scolded.

The attendant shrugged. 'I am the Royal announcer, not a Royal deliverer.'

I was beginning to see that job roles were taken very literally here. It was no wonder they had to introduce the games. I could easily see Finn getting a little stabby if someone tried to usurp his new role.

'Never mind,' I said, picking the lid up and putting it back on top of the box. 'I won't be wearing that. Let's go as we are.'

The two attendants who had dragged the dress-box up the steps looked daggers at me for a moment, before turning on their heels and beginning their long decent.

'Shall I give that message to our king?' asked the Royal announcer.

'Yes, please do,' I said.

***

I had to send away a hairdresser, and an attendant carrying a box of heavy, expensive-looking jewellery before the afternoon was over. I had to admit, I felt a little guilty, but I knew it would all be worth it to see Heston's face when he realised his Royal witch wasn't going to play any of his games.

LIFE'S A WITCH

Finn, on the other hand, had disappeared for an hour to 'get his glad rags on'. When he met up with me again, outside the throne room, he was wearing an adapted version of his usual red and black uniform, except that it was shot through with glitter. There were gemstones twisted into his red hair, and a chain of diamonds draped around his neck.

'You look... very sparkly,' I said as a way of greeting.

'Just say I look good, or don't say anything at all,' he complained.

'You look good,' I agreed.

'You look terrible, to be honest,' he said bluntly. 'I see what you're trying to do, but you could have changed.' He looked me up and down, shaking his head. 'It's just bad manners.'

'I didn't have anything else!' I complained. 'It was bad manners of the king to force me here without letting me pack any of my own clothes!'

'Alright, alright,' said Finn, placing a calming hand on my shoulder. 'Let's just go in.'

I nodded to the two guards stationed in front of us, signalling that we were ready, and they immediately opened the doors.

The throne room was as beautiful as ever, decorated with long, draping garlands full of bright red roses.

A black, velvet carpet was rolled out down the middle of the room, leading from the door up to the dais. The guests stood either side, all dressed in elaborate costumes. The women wore dresses of sparkling silver-plated armour, while the men were dressed in black and white robes that were dripping with diamonds and gemstones. Some guests had ornate weapons. I saw broadswords, strapped at hips, that were so highly decorated that they weren't fit for purpose. One woman, in a long, shimmering gown, was carrying a long bow over her shoulder. It was taller than she was, and wrapped in red ribbons that trailed along the floor as she walked.

An attendant by the door announced my name as I stepped onto the black carpet. Finn stood behind me, hands clasped together and head slightly down. Was he playing the part of a modest Royal attendant?

At the announcement, all eyes turned my way, and I felt a little nervous. I looked down at my feet, but that made the feeling worse, as I realised my brown boots were stained with various colours of potion that I had spilled over the years, and, as always, carried a thick layer of magic dust.

Finn came and stood beside me, noticing my hesitation.

'You've got this, Hedgehog,' he whispered. 'You're the most powerful witch in the room, so hold your head up high. They will all be begging their seamstresses for a copy of your dress tomorrow.' He squeezed my shoulder reassuringly and I smiled back at him. He was alright, really.

I walked down the carpet towards the dais with purpose, but I had to admit I almost faltered to a complete stop when I saw Heston.

LIFE'S A WITCH

He was sitting upon a throne of shimmering gold, a pattern of roses and thorns etched out in black all along it.

The king sat effortlessly. His legs were crossed lazily over one of the arms and his chin was resting elegantly in his hand. He was wearing a black suit, shot through with gold, and a robe of translucent, shimmering black draped down from his shoulders, to pool on the floor around him. His hair was loose and messy, flowing down over his shoulders. The crown was crooked on Heston's head, giving him a dishevelled air.

He was mesmerising, exactly as you would expect of a vampire king. His eyes were flecked with gold, and his lips were full and slightly red, as though he had just been kissing someone.

Had he?

Why did I care if he had? I barely knew the man, and he was a complete flirt.

He watched me intently as I approached, ignoring the attendant at his side, who was trying to pass him a goblet.

I stared back, meeting his ruby red gaze. It felt bold to meet his eyes.

I tried desperately to ignore the sickening butterflies in my stomach, and hoped he couldn't tell how nervous and excited he made me feel.

He smiled at me then, his face transforming as he stood up in one fast, fluid motion. I knew that, had I attempted the same move, I would have tangled myself up in the tulle cape and ended up on the floor.

He stepped down from the dais and approached me. I stopped, as my treacherous heart skipped a beat.

Finn bowed low beside me as Heston came to a stop in front of us. I was aware of the crowds of people either side, watching our exchange with interest.

'Dear Hodge, you are a vision tonight,' said Heston, with a wicked smile.

'Do you like it?' I asked, as I summoned up the courage to do a little twirl. This vampire could look as unshakable as he wanted, but surely I had struck a nerve by sending back all of his dresses?

'I do,' he said, his voice low, as his sharp stare followed my every movement.

I wished he would stop looking at me like I was dinner.

I stopped twirling, feeling a little deflated by his reaction.

'Shall I introduce you to my uncle properly?' he asked, holding out an arm for me to take. 'You have already met the winner of our games this evening.' He pointed out Grant, who was sitting in a chair on the dais, a chair that was much too small for him. He had a gold medal around his neck and was looking very pleased with himself.

'He wanted to be my Royal General,' Heston whispered low, leaning in close. 'But I managed to convince him to be Head of Battle instead.'

'And what is that?' I asked. Heston shrugged and smiled conspiratorially.

'Who knows?' he replied. 'I'll have to think of something.'

I tried to shoot him a scornful stare, but I couldn't muster it. I wasn't very fond of Grant, probably something to do with him almost flattening me.

Yet, as I watched him, happily drinking and showing off his medal to the crowds, I felt a little guilty, so I shot Heston an even sterner stare. As usual, that seemed to amuse him.

Goddess forbid I were actually nice to the man, he would probably tire of me in an instant.

Actually, that could be an idea…

'Uncle Trevor, you have met my Royal wizard, Hedgehog.'

'I have,' said the uncle, who was standing close to the throne, looking very big and very regal.

'Hello, again,' I said.

'So, here we are,' he said, smiling down at me kindly. 'Me, the oldest member of this court, and you, the newest,' he continued. 'I think that is as good a reason as any for us to open the ceremony?' He held out a hand to me.

I looked at Heston, unsure, before placing my hand into Trevor's. Heston clicked his tongue and shook his head. It seemed playful, but I noticed a tick in his jaw and I was sure he held my other arm a fraction tighter.

'What a charming notion, Uncle, though I am not sure Grant would agree,' Heston said. 'As the winner of the games, he had asked to open the dancing. With me.' Grant stood up then, having clearly overheard the conversation.

'Before that, though!' cried Heston, addressing the entire room. 'In her first act as Royal wizard...' He guided me so that I was at the very front of the dais, with all eyes on me. 'Our witch will announce the dates for our ending ceremony, and for the long-awaited Pumpkin Ball!'

The crowd cheered as two attendants approached me, one carrying a bronze telescopic alidade, the other holding a heavy tome and quill. A small table was procured from somewhere and slammed down in front of me.

I looked at Heston blankly as I accepted the alidade.

'What am I doing?' I asked him quietly.

'Setting the date for the ceremonies,' he replied. 'Just look at the stars and tell us what dates are prosperous.' He spoke flippantly, as though it was something any witch would be able to do.

'Uh, I've never been very good with astronomy,' I said. Heston stared at me a moment, stunned, and then threw his head back and laughed.

'I'm starting to think you weren't the right choice for this job,' he said.

'I'm not,' I hissed back. 'Fire me now, before it's too late.'

'Never.'

'I told you that you overestimated me,' I complained, as Heston gently moved me so that I was standing in the middle of the dais.

LIFE'S A WITCH

'Just point the instrument up through that glass window,' he said, as he tilted my head up so that I could see that he was right. A glass window above gave a direct view into the night sky.

'Fake it, dear Hodge,' he whispered, his hand still clasping my chin. 'Any day is as good as the next.'

I shuffled away from him and fiddled about with the alidade a bit. It gave a loud click, as if something had dropped inside. I was quite sure at this point that it was broken. I pointed it up at the sky, anyway.

'Wrong way,' Heston whispered, quickly taking it from me and turning it around.

'I knew that,' I said. 'I was testing you.' I looked up at the stars. It was a clear night and the view was beautiful. A witch with a lot more experience than me would have found it fascinating. Even Morgan would have known more about this than I did.

I watched as a shooting star flew down, a red trail blazing behind it. I moved the alidade and lined it up with the star, but I really had no idea what I was doing. I had never used equipment like this. I had read about it in books before my initiation, but never in practice.

Scrying would be easier for me.

I put the device down on the floor and grabbed the quill ink.

I gestured for Heston to back up a bit, which he did. He took a seat on the dais steps, watching me with interest.

I drew out a circle on the floor. The black ink was stark in contrast to the white marble and I really hoped it would wash off.

'Finn, can you get me a bowl of water, please?' I asked the attendant. He nodded his head and rushed off.

I pulled some stones from my pocket and placed them at north, south, east and west as offerings of thanks to the goddess.

Finn came back with a small porcelain bowl, filled to the brim with crystal clear water.

'Will this work?' he asked. I nodded as I took the bowl and placed it down in the middle of the circle.

Then, I sat cross-legged in front of the bowl and closed the circle with one last stroke of the pen, enclosing myself and the bowl inside.

'Don't step inside,' I warned, as Uncle Trevor leant down to inspect the circle. He held his hands up in apology and moved backward.

I shut my eyes and focused on releasing my magic into the air. I could feel the tendrils unravelling from my body and reaching out for the bowl.

'Show me,' I whispered. I opened my eyes and stared deep into the bowl, which was now tinged bright green by my magic. I could see a party in the waters. People dancing and spinning quickly, no one that I recognised.

'When?' I urged, allowing more magic to flow from my body and into the water.

LIFE'S A WITCH

The view panned up, showing the moon waxing gibbous. Then it panned back down in a fast spiral, making me dizzy. The water darkened and I could see a vision of Trevor, leaning over me. His eyes were blood red and full of malice as he loomed closer. I felt a choking feeling in my chest. I quickly reached out and tipped the bowl over, spilling black water all over the circle.

I leant over and used my skirts to brush the ink lines away, opening the circle, before quickly standing and walking out. The whole room was silent and watching me. Heston had approached and was standing as close to the circle as he dared, a look of concern on his face.

I tried to smile, but felt quite drained.

'The ceremony should be under the moon waxing gibbous,' I said, trying to keep my voice calm and steady, while I keenly felt the presence of Uncle Trevor closing in on me.

'Waxing gibbous?' Heston asked.

I looked up at the sky. It was still a quarter moon, but the waxing moon would be any day.

'Only a few days,' I explained. 'So, next Friday?'

'And the Pumpkin Ball?' asked Grant, who had been watching the entire thing with excitement.

Shit, I had completely forgotten to look that one up.

'Uh, on the same day!' I cried, unsure. I heard Heston let out a small chuckle beside me.

'Do you hear that, all?' he cried to the room. 'The dates have been decided.' He picked up the quill from the floor, opened the large tome and added the dates at the bottom of what was already an extremely long list of dates.

'And now,' he said, as he slammed the book shut again. 'We dance!'

Chapter 12

It would take a little while for me to forget the image of Grant and Heston gliding elegantly across the ballroom floor together. Grant certainly didn't look like the type to be so nimble, and yet it had been a beautiful sight. I wasn't the only one who felt such awe. Uncle Trevor had stood next to me, watching in silence also. He didn't seem to remember that he had asked me for a dance until long after Heston and Grant had moved on to new partners. He did remember, however, just as the music shifted to a much more jaunty tune.

I hopped and stumbled around in circles with the large vampire, feeling every bit as awkward as I must have looked. Trevor, though, to his credit, plastered on a large smile and didn't say anything unpleasant, even when I stood on his feet, or accidently rammed my knee directly into his crotch.

'I feel I may have ruined your spell,' said Trevor, apologetically.

'Oh?' I prompted, carefully focusing on trying not to fall and not really taking in his words.

'I forgot myself and leant over into the circle,' he explained.

'What?' I asked, confused.

'I was so interested,' he continued. 'I made sure not to step over the line, as you said, but I did lean. When I saw my reflection in the water, I knew that I had gone too far, and done wrong. I can only apologise to you, and hope that my actions didn't ruin your prediction.'

I stared at the vampire, dumbfounded by his confession. It took a few more seconds for me to process what he was saying and its implications.

Surely not?

Had the vision of Trevor, looming over me so maliciously, actually just been Trevor... looming over me?

I looked up at the vampire again. He was watching me intently, searching my face, waiting to see if I would reprimand or redeem him.

'Uh, don't worry about it,' I said, feeling unsure of myself.

His expression shifted instantly from one of apprehension, to a relieved and open smile.

'I was concerned, as it is very important to get these things right,' he said, making me feel more than a little guilty about completely making up the date of the Pumpkin Ball.

LIFE'S A WITCH

I didn't have to respond, because just then the tempo of the music began to speed up. Trevor raised his arm and directed me into a turn. He didn't stop at just one turn, though, as I had expected. He spun me around, over and over again, to the point where I knew I was going to fall over the very moment he stopped.

Except, that I didn't fall, because a strong pair of hands encircled my waist and held me tightly until the room stopped spinning and the nausea subsided. When I felt more stable, I turned to see Heston was the one holding me.

'May I cut in?' he asked.

Trevor nodded, looking a little bit disappointed. He hesitated a moment, before bowing to me and letting go of my hand. As he walked away, he shot me a glance.

I couldn't say what that look was about. Perhaps he had wanted to ask more about my divination circle?

'Do you need to sit down?' Heston breathed in my ear, his arms still holding me steady.

I shook my head, sending the room back into a little spin.

'Then, will you dance with me?'

I nodded, wordlessly, feeling suddenly nervous. I didn't like the way Heston made me feel. It was an odd mix of nausea and thrill, but there was also something about him that made me feel safe.

'You look beautiful,' he said, as he rested his hands on my hips.

'Really?' I asked. 'I didn't have anything else to wear.'

I watched his reaction, expecting him to smile politely again. But there was an odd look in his eyes, like maybe he was… hurt?

'I couldn't get your clothes here in time. I apologise..' he said, sincerely.

'You should have let me bring them,' I scolded as the music started up again and we began to sway gently. I let Heston lead, and was relieved that we were taking it slowly. I looked around to see the other couples following suit and adjusting their movement to ours.

'We didn't have time,' he said. 'We only just made it to the ball. Do you not recall?'

'Then you should have left me at the shoppe,' I said, refusing to give in.

'Well, perhaps I should have,' he conceded. 'Perhaps if I hadn't tried to force things, my father would still be alive now.'

I felt the shock of guilt at his words.

'I don't think it was my fault,' I said, trying to convince myself as much as him. 'But I am very sorry that it happened.'

'Thank you.'

'Was he a good man?' I asked. Heston was silent and thoughtful for a moment as he guided me gently around the ballroom.

'I think so,' he answered eventually. 'He was stubborn, but he was good to me.'

LIFE'S A WITCH

'Has there been a...' I was going to ask if there had been an autopsy done on the king, but I couldn't get the words out. It didn't seem like the sort of question to ask right now, and I had to admit that I was a little worried about the answer.

I hadn't taken a moment since it happened to wonder about the possibility that I had actually caused the king's death. It hadn't occurred to me, because it just didn't seem possible.

But, of course, it was possible. I had used my mother's spell, without knowing all the ingredients, and without even a second thought.

However, I had sensed its intent, and there had been nothing malicious about it. It was an enhancing potion and nothing more, I was sure of that.

'Don't look so worried, Hodge,' Heston send gently. 'We will get to the bottom of it, eventually. It is common for kings to go this way. My grandfather was poisoned, too, you know, and the culprit was never found.' He said this so conversationally, like it was a normal part of his life.

'I'm sorry,' I said, because what else could I say?

'Don't be. I don't blame you,' he breathed.

We danced in silence then, and with every passing moment I became more hyper-aware of his firm grip on my hips, and the closeness of his body. The air around us began to feel charged, and my magic crackled at my fingertips. I looked up, to see if he had noticed, and my stomach lurched to find him watching me intently, his ruby red gaze exploring my face, my eyes, my lips.

'You are beautiful,' he said, so softly that I almost didn't hear it. He lifted his hand and ran it through my messy hair, brushing it away from my face and twisting it in his fingers until it curled.

The music came to an end and, wordlessly, I pulled away from the vampire. I cursed him under my breath as I stomped back down the black carpet, eager to be as far away from him as possible.

I was starting to feel like I couldn't trust myself around this vampire.

I needed to get a grip. I wasn't some teenager with a crush, and Heston was not the type I could risk getting involved with.

Just before I reached the doors, Heston grabbed a hold of my wrist, stopping me and pulling me to face him.

'What are you doing?' he demanded.

'Let me go.'

'Why?' he asked. His face was a mask, and I couldn't tell what he was thinking.

'I know you find it fun to toy with me,' I said, breathlessly. 'But I'm not used to it, and it makes me uncomfortable.'

'Toy with you?' he repeated, his brows furrowing. 'Explain.'

'The touching, and the flirting. I don't like it,' I said. My face blushed furiously and I looked down at the floor, unable to meet his eyes.

'You didn't mind when that witch did it, so why is it an issue with me?' he asked, his voice low and dark.

What witch? Surely he didn't mean Cole? There wasn't anyone else, unless he had been watching me for a while? But I doubted that.

'Cole is harmless. He is a childhood friend and his playful teasing is nothing compared to the things you say and do. ' I rebuffed. Heston smiled wickedly.

'Do you think that, maybe, you enjoy it more when I do it, and that's why it makes you uncomfortable?' he asked. 'Besides, it would only be classed as "toying" if I was playing with you. Which I am not. I think we have chemistry, Hodge, don't you?'

I stared up at him, speechless for a moment.

'No,' I lied.

'What are you afraid of?' he asked, looking frustrated.

'You!' I snapped. 'I'm afraid of you, and I don't want to be your plaything. I want to go back to my little shoppe, and be left well alone.'

He looked at me, surprised by my outburst. I took that moment to pull free. When I reached the doors, the guards stationed there looked over my head, refusing to open them without Heston's approval.

SIMONE NATALIE

Just more affirmation that I was a prisoner.
'Let her go,' Heston yelled, angrily.
I wished he would.

Chapter 13

When I got back to the tower, it was to find Finn, and several other attendants, attempting to push a large mattress up the winding tower steps.

I slipped past them easily, ignoring a few choice words from Finn.

As I reached the phoenix stone, it glowed a bright gold in greeting.

'Hello, Nixie,' I replied, rubbing my hands along the sparkling green gemstone as I passed by. Nixie seemed like a cute nickname and, since it didn't turn me into smoke or dust, I presumed the phoenix had no problem with it. I made it a rule to always presume sentience, or else you could find yourself getting undressed in front of what you presume is a mirror, but is actually a bespelled goblin.

I was exhausted, and just wanted to collapse on the window seat to sleep.

That wouldn't be happening, however, as the attendants had been very busy while I was dancing the night away. The tower room was gutted of most of its furniture, and was in the process of being completely rearranged.

All the paperwork that had littered the floors was stacked into neat piles, or large wooden crates. The floor and table were clear of the debris and bric-a-brac that the wizard had left behind.

The four-poster bed had been stripped to its frame and an attendant was busy wrapping new fabric around the beams. It was deep purple in colour, decorated with bright sparkles that shimmered like stars underneath the glowing light of the chandelier.

'That's beautiful,' I breathed in awe and I couldn't stop myself from reaching over to touch the fabric. It was thick and soft.

'His Holy Darkness ordered it for you, to match the carpet,' replied the attendant.

'What carpet?' I asked.

The attendant pointed towards the large table in the middle of the tower room where, underneath, lay a perfect oval cut-out of my carpet. The one from my store room, complete with a thick layer of my spell dust.

LIFE'S A WITCH

The edges of the carpet had been re-trimmed in a purple fabric, with handsewn patterns in the shape of moons, planets and constellations. It was stunning.

My heart throbbed a little as I looked at it. I tried to push the feeling down, reminding myself what a complete fuckwit the vampire king was. But I was touched and I couldn't pretend it away.

'I have to go home,' I stammered out as an odd fear gripped me.

'What?'

I jumped. Finn had snuck up beside me without my noticing, despite his breathing heavily from having to hoist the mattress up the stairs.

'What did you say?' he panted.

'Uh, I have to go home.'

'This is your home,' he said firmly.

That was what I was afraid of.

Heston had noticed how important my spell dust was, and how I would need it with me to perform my spells. It gave me the impression that he really thought I would be staying here… indefinitely.

'This is your home,' repeated Finn, looking uncharacteristically stern. 'Or else, why did I just half-kill myself pulling this mattress up those hell-forsaken stairs? He did it to punish me, you know. For allowing you to fight. A simple float spell would have…' He trailed off as he looked more closely at my face.

'You look a little peaky,' he said.

'I feel it.'

Finn pulled a chair out from under the table, just in time for me to collapse into it.

'It's hitting you now, huh?' he said comfortingly. 'Maybe you were in a bit of shock.'

'Maybe I was.'

'Well, you didn't expect to kill the vampire king and get to just stroll on home afterwards? Did you?'

'Wait, what do you know?' I gasped.

'Oh, please, everyone knows,' replied Finn. 'There are no secrets here, everything is in the walls.' He gestured around vaguely. 'No, really. The walls talk. Those damn paintings are such gossips. If it was up to me…'

I couldn't listen anymore. I stood up and made to escape to the stairs, only to find my way barred by a handful of attendants, carrying what could only be described as the contents of my entire life.

My broom floated past my head and settled itself next to a bookshelf, quickly followed by my large cauldron, bobbing along chaotically, until it settled with a loud crash into the fireplace, completely crushing the old wizard's cauldron to dust beneath it. Enchanted bottles and papers whizzed past my head to settle themselves into any vacated spot where they could fit, and attendants began to slot my books onto the shelves, alongside those of the wizard's.

LIFE'S A WITCH

I felt a bit dizzy, and my heart leapt around in my chest as my entire wardrobe loomed at the top of the stairs. It teetered a little, before toppling over the threshold and crawling over to replace the old wardrobe. I quickly ran over and pointed for it to place itself next to it, instead of on top, like the cauldron had. I turned back, feeling even more frazzled when the vampire king himself strode in.

It hadn't been an hour since I had left him, and my stomach swooped for a moment, wondering why he was here. He didn't look like his usual unfazed self. His hair was chaotic, strands of it tangled up in his crown. The hem of his cloak was thick in dust. And he looked a little flushed, almost as though he had made haste up those tower stairs.

He met my eyes for a moment, and my stomach swooped. He opened his mouth to say something, but just then a dining room chair from my kitchen at the shoppe swooped in front of him and landed at the round table, shuffling to squeeze between the chairs already placed there.

I looked back at Heston to see him biting his lip and frowning. However, the moment he met my eyes, the look faded into his usual ease.

'Are you pleased with it?' he asked, spreading his arms out and admiring the room. 'I wanted to make you feel more at home,' he continued, looking earnest.

I nodded awkwardly. My mouth felt dry and my heart was palpitating uncomfortably in my chest.

Heston's smile dropped. 'I can see that my generosity has left you speechless,' he said sarcastically. He looked genuinely disappointed by my lacklustre reaction. 'Can we talk, Hodge?' He hesitated a moment, then he slid his hand along my hip and pulled me closer.

'What's wrong?' he asked, his voice low.

'I don't want to be here,' I answered, honestly.

To give him credit, he didn't flinch. Instead, he stared at me steadily in silence, as if to weigh the truth in my words. His crimson eyes flicked across my face, taking in every worried frown line hidden there.

'We made a deal,' Heston said eventually. 'The Manor has already claimed you.' He twisted a strand of my hair between his slender fingers. 'The Manor let you in, trusted you, showed you its true self,' he continued, his voice cracking slightly as he dropped to a whisper. 'Leaving now won't be easy. You made a commitment, Hodge.' He looked hauntingly beautiful to me now, and a small, traitorous part of me wanted to nod and agree and apologise for ever thinking of leaving this wild, chaotic place.

But, that part wasn't strong enough to change my mind.

I didn't want to be a prisoner.

I took a step backwards, distancing myself. The strands of hair slipped from Heston's fingers. He cleared his throat and walked over to a large cabinet, that was filled entirely with the wizard's dusty books.

LIFE'S A WITCH

His fingers trailed along the decaying volumes until he reached a small, leather-bound book. In one flick of his wrist, he nudged the top of the tome, causing it to tumble forward onto its spine.

Heston shot me a slow, meaningful look, before clicking his tongue, turning away and disappearing back down the tower staircase. I watched until the top of his black-as-pitch hair vanished.

The bustle of the room came back into stark focus as I realised there were still attendants hurrying around me, clearing up, decorating and placing my items among those of Frank's that still remained. The feeling of guilt returned to the pit of my stomach. I had no right to take over the wizard's home, on nothing but the authority of Heston's whim.

With trepidation, I walked over to the shelves and slid the book out that Heston had dropped.

A few pages flew out and splayed along the floor. The pages were browned and stained with age. The words within were handwritten in a messy, small scribble. I quickly picked up the scattered pages and placed them back in haphazardly.

'That's Frank's journal,' Finn said, as he crept up next to me to inspect the book. 'They all are.' He waved at the bookcase in front of me, indicating the rows upon row of books. 'Is this volume important?'

'Maybe,' I answered as I turned it over in my hands in awe. How could one man fill so many books? 'How old *is* the wizard?' I asked. Finn shrugged.

'How long is a piece of string?' he replied, as if that was answer enough.

I sighed and sat down on the nearest chair, feeling drained all of a sudden. The book slipped out of my grip and landed on the floor. Finn frowned in concern.

'It's very late,' he said. 'Come try out your bed, see if you like it?'

I let him lead me over to the bed, where the attendant had finished her draping and another was plumping up the pillows. Finn ordered them away with a wave of his hand, and I sank down into the soft mattress. I hated to admit it, but it was much more comfortable than my bed at home. I rolled over and stared out of the glass windows at the twinkling city lights in the distance.

Chapter 14

I awoke to chirping birdsong and bright autumn sunlight. I could hear Finn's voice nearby, and the smell of coffee roused me.

'How did you sleep?' Finn asked from my bedside. I sat up and looked around in a daze. It was full daylight outside so I must have slept for hours.

'What time is it?' I croaked as I took the coffee he was offering.

'Getting late,' he admitted. 'They have already served lunch.' He waved a hand at the table, where lay a porcelain tray full of sandwiches, pastries, cheeses and crackers, jars of chutney and a large silver teapot.

My stomach growled. I drew back the covers and made my way over.

Just then, there was a clambering by the stairs as a tall, green-skinned attendant appeared, looking very worn out.

'Forgive my intrusion, oh witchlyness,' the attendant panted.

'Yes, what is it?' asked Finn haughtily. I got the feeling that his appointment as my attendant was going to his head a little.

'There is a visitor at the Manor door, who is insisting on seeing the Royal witch.'

'Who?' I asked, as an anxious feeling seeped into my chest.

'He gave his name as Kid.'

Morgan!

I dropped the sandwich that had made it halfway to my mouth, and ran.

As I raced down the steps, almost tripping over my own feet, I realised I had no idea where the main door was, or how to get there.

Oh, wait. I was so *stupid*.

I ran to the nearest door and stared up at it, feeling a little foolish.

'Can you please take me to the main entrance?' I asked hurriedly. I opened the door to walk through, then stopped dead, thinking better of it. My last run-in with one of these doors had ended in a broken ankle and I wasn't keen for a repeat.

'Actually,' I said resolutely, shutting the door again. 'Take me *right* to Morgan, no tricks! Just drop me off as close as I can get,' I said very firmly, rapping on the wood sharply with my athame for good measure. Politeness had got me nowhere before, so maybe these doors needed a firmer hand. 'And, if you don't do exactly as I ask, I will tell the king!'

Without any further hesitation, I pulled open the door and raced through.

It slammed shut behind me and I found myself in a small library. There was a large, open fireplace with a crackling fire, and a beautiful bay window with a tray, upon which was a cup of tea. A book lay upended, as though someone had been disturbed and hastily set it down.

I looked around frantically, searching the handful of plush armchairs gathered around the fire. I had almost decided that the door had messed with me again, when I was startled by a voice from directly above me.

'We're up here!' I looked up and saw Heston leaning over a balcony. He was stirring something in a small teacup, his expression unreadable. He took out the small silver spoon, tapped it on the edge of the cup and pointed it in the direction of a narrow, circular staircase that I hadn't spotted before now.

Great, so Heston had already found him.

I nodded and ran over to the stairs, rushing up to the second level, which was just a small, open room that looked down over the rest of the library. There was a round side table, with a tea tray and cake stand layered with deserts. And, in one of the plush red armchairs perched Morgan, awkwardly. He was clasping an untouched Cherry Bakewell in his hands, and looked visibly relieved to see me.

'What are you doing here, Kid?' I asked as I raced over to him. 'Are you okay?' I took the Bakewell, tossing it onto the table, and knelt down to his level.

'Are you okay?' I repeated.

'I should be asking you that!' he snapped. His glasses were slightly askew and his curly hair was tangled, like he had been running his hands through it in worry. 'What were you *thinking?*' he continued, glaring at me with the same scolding look I had used on him countless times. 'Wandering off all alone, to a vampire castle of all places, without even telling us where you were going!'

'How did you find me?' I asked.

'Mum had to scry!' His face was flushed red as a result of anger, relief and yelling.

'Calm down, Morgan, I'll explain. Wait..' I stopped. 'Raven *scryed?*' I asked, shocked.

He nodded emphatically.

'Your mum scryed?'

'Yes!' he replied, frustrated. 'Every time I tried it, the location was too broad and I couldn't narrow it down enough.' He looked a little disappointed in himself.

'It's because you aren't initiated yet,' I said.

'Well, whatever,' said Morgan, brushing it off. 'But we couldn't reach Granny, either, and we didn't know if it was safe to tell the coven. So Mum *had* to do it, there was no one else.'

'I said not to scry…' I began.

He looked at me with his eyebrows drawn and his lips pinched together in annoyance. It was a look he got from his grandmother, for sure.

'And after that weird feeling I got… and the way you quickly got me out of the way… You knew what was going to happen. It's because of the potion, isn't it?' he asked.

I quickly put my finger to my lips and shot a warning look towards Heston from the corner of my eye.

Morgan looked for all the world like he had completely forgotten about the vampire prince. He leant back in his chair and pursed his lips closed tight, as if he could take back what he had already said.

'It doesn't matter,' I said, as I cleared my throat and stood up, brushing non-existent dust from my clothes out of habit. 'You have seen me now, so you have to go home and tell your mum to stop worrying.'

'Aunt H, I am not going anywhere without you,' Morgan said, firmly.

Until now, Heston had been silently observing us both from his armchair, while sipping on his tea and looking seemingly uninterested. He uncrossed his legs in a slow, effortless motion and stood up from his chair. He picked up the Bakewell cake I had thrown onto the table and placed it down again onto a delicate China tea plate.

'No manners, dear witch,' he scolded gently, in that annoying, beautiful voice. 'There are crumbs all over my table.'

My face flushed in annoyance. 'You had your feet on my dinner table last week, so what are you talking about?' I snapped. The vampire clicked his tongue scoldingly, flicking his eyes in my direction.

'There's a reason for that,' he said, softly. 'Crumbs have no reason.'

'And what was the reason?' I hissed, knowing it was going to be something stupid. He ignored me entirely, however, instead fixing Morgan with a kind, disarming smile and handing the plate over to him. Morgan took it, hesitantly.

'You *must* stay, dear Morgan,' Heston said sincerely. I wanted to spell him, right then and there. He would make a lovely frog. 'Family to my witch, is family to me,' he continued. 'Besides, you have come at the perfect time for me to show off all that my home has to offer, what with the games in full swing, and the Pumpkin Ball approaching. It would be uncivilised of me to turn away a guest at this time.'

'He is not staying, Heston,' I said, approaching the vampire with my most stern witch glare. I even let my magic crackle in the air a little for good measure. Unfortunately, as always, Heston seemed more charmed by my attempts at threatening him than anything else. He smiled tenderly at me and reached out to touch a little green zip of magic. He shivered from the electric shock as it made contact. He inspected his slightly singed fingers with interest.

'No harm will come to your nephew while he is under my care,' he said solemnly, and he traced a cross over his heart with his fingers. 'So don't worry.'

'Swear it!' I said through gritted teeth. 'Swear you won't let him come to harm!'

At this, Heston looked happier than ever and his eyes darkened as he fixed me with a dangerous grin.

'You want me to swear?' he asked.

'Yes.'

'Morgan, dear,' he said, not taking his eyes from my face as he addressed my nephew. 'Please go down to the library and fetch me my notebook. It's in the left-hand drawer of my desk.'

'Okay...' Morgan replied, sounding very unsure. I heard his steps retreating down the small, creaking steps, nonetheless. I didn't look away from the vampire. I wanted him to understand how important this was.

'Swear it, Heston,' I repeated, as my eyes burnt into his.

'I swear,' he breathed, holding his hand out for me to take. I hesitated, but reached out and placed my hand on his. As he gripped it, hard, his eyes widened and I knew what he was going to do, a second too late to stop it.

He pulled me so that our bodies where flush and wrapped his free arm around my waist, forcing us closer still. Slowly, wordlessly, he lifted my hand up to his mouth and brushed his lips along my inner wrist gently. He shut his eyes and breathed in, the soft touch on my sensitive inner wrist sending shivers up and down my spine.

A large part of me knew I should try to pull away, or at least protest. Yet, I had a sick, exciting sense of anticipation for what was coming.

Heston's gaze flicked up and his eyes met mine. He stared at me, watching my reaction, waiting for my approval.

I nodded my head ever so slightly, which was agreement enough for him. With a low sigh, he opened his mouth. I saw a flash of fangs before he sunk them deep into my inner wrist.

I flinched, expecting pain, but instead a pleasant tingle ran through my body. He smiled slyly at my reaction, catching my eye as he lifted his head. He looked almost drunk, his eyes glassy. There was something dishevelled about him now that I could see his fangs. His smile seemed dangerous and shockingly beautiful.

I tried to pull my arm away, suddenly ashamed, but he held it tighter, clicking his tongue scoldingly as he pulled it up. I followed, suddenly face to face with him. I could feel my heart beating too fast, and I flushed at the realisation that he could also hear it.

'Always seal a promise in blood,' he whispered, looking hungrily at my mouth.

I don't know what came over me then, but I leant in and softly touched my lips against his. It was only for the length of a heartbeat.

I pulled back, quickly, fully realising what I had done.

Heston blinked at me, his eyes flared in surprise.

'Hodge,' he breathed.

It sounded like a warning.

His irises deepened to a darker shade of red an instant before he crushed his lips to mine. I gasped and pulled back, only to wrap my arms around his neck. He let out an appreciative noise and kissed me again, desperately. His hands became tangled up in my hair, and our teeth clashed as we kissed.

I couldn't breathe. My heart was hammering and I felt dizzy. I swayed slightly in his arms and he lifted me up, so that my toes were barely touching the floor.

'The drawer is locked!' Morgan's words calling up from the bottom of the stairs snapped me from my momentary madness and I jumped back hurriedly, shocked and embarrassed.

Morgan's fast footfalls reached the top of the steps. 'I couldn't find the key,' he said.

Heston stared at my nephew, his expression dark and muddled, as though he couldn't understand what was being said. In an instant it was gone, replaced with a mask of calm.

'Ah, no matter,' he said. 'I don't need my notebook now.' His voice was coarser than usual, and I felt a slight satisfaction in knowing that he felt every bit as frazzled as I did. That was quickly followed by a wave of pure panic. What was I *thinking*?

Morgan finished his ascent up the stairs and looked at us both suspiciously, sensing that something wasn't right.

'What happened?' he asked me. 'Did something happen?'

I shook my head reassuringly, not trusting myself to speak. Self-conscious all of a sudden, I tried to cover my blood-smudged wrist with my sleeve, pulling it down as far as it would go.

'Everything is fine,' said Heston. 'It has been agreed that you will stay until you are convinced that your aunt is being well looked after.'

'I will stay, until she comes back with me,' Morgan said, crossing his arms stubbornly.

Heston chose to ignore this remark. Instead, he held his hand out, signalling for Morgan to go back down the steps.

'I will get you set up with a bedroom,' he said, 'and an attendant to show you around and make sure you don't get lost.'

Morgan shot me a look of concern and started down the steps. Heston held back, turning to me.

He opened his mouth to say something, but I shook my head and dashed down the stairs ahead of him, making sure not to touch him as I slipped past. I didn't want to hear anything from him. I didn't even want to look at him right now.

I had to make it my mission to never let *that* happen *ever* again!

Chapter 15

'What is your name?' asked Finn when we were all sitting at the tower table later that evening.

'No, don't!' I warned.

'Morgan,' answered my nephew at the same time. I cursed myself for not warning him before I introduced them both. It's not like I thought Finn would, or even *could*, do anything with the name, but you never knew with fairies.

'That is a good name,' said Finn, looking thoughtful. 'Very dark.'

'Why's that?' asked Morgan, perplexed. 'Does it have a meaning?' He looked at me, as if I would know. I shrugged. I was pretty sure Raven had just liked the sound of it. When she chose Morgan's name, she had broken the longstanding Broome tradition of naming our children after animals.

I couldn't blame her.

'Morgan, morgue and organ,' explained Finn.

'Yeah, I don't think that's what my mum was going for,' Morgan laughed.

'Are you drunk?' I asked Finn, half-jokingly. As I spoke, I realised he was swaying side to side on the wooden chair.

'Yes, a little,' he replied. 'It's my birthday today, so me and some friends had a little party earlier.'

'Happy birthday, Finn!' I cried. 'You should have said something!'

'About what?' he asked blankly.

'Oh, this guy is wasted,' Morgan chuckled.

'You had a party?' I sulked, jokingly. 'Why wasn't I invited?'

'I couldn't find you,' he said simply.

That was probably the truth, since I had spent the most part of the day trying to convince Morgan to leave, while simultaneously trying to convince Heston to kick him out. Neither had budged, and now Morgan was settled in a bedroom in the west wing.

'I think it's very rude not to include friends in important plans,' stated Morgan's new attendant. 'I never get invited to parties.'

In what was almost certainly a thinly disguised punishment, Morgan's attendant was none other than the older lady he had first sold the potion to. Her name was Elizabeth, and she wasn't very pleasant, actually. She sat in her chair, eating a cucumber sandwich and glowering at us all.

'Calm down, Beth,' Finn slurred. 'I will invite you next time.' He turned directly to me and, in what he must have thought was a whisper, said very loudly, 'That was a lie. I would never invite her.' Beth glared at the tipsy fairy and Morgan laughed nervously from behind his teacup.

'I was almost queen, you know,' she snapped. Finn shook his head at this and laughed so hard that he toppled off his chair.

'If only you hadn't sold me a dud spell,' she hissed at Morgan angrily, before turning her gaze up to the ceiling with a dazed, faraway look. 'I could be queen right now, and lying in bed with that sexy vampire, doing—'

'Well, that's probably enough of that,' I cut in, standing up and making a point of placing the used cups and plates back onto the tray.

Beth snapped out of her daydream and continued glaring at Morgan. 'I want my money back,' she growled.

A flash of lightning made us all jump. It lit up the entire dome, and was quickly followed by a crash of thunder.

'Oh, that sounds nasty,' said Finn, as the window was showered with heavy rain, causing a loud pitter patter to resound throughout the tower room.

'I think now is as good a time as any to call it a night,' I said, anxious to get rid of Beth.

'I'm pretty tired,' Morgan agreed.

LIFE'S A WITCH

'Are you going to be alright?' I asked him, pulling him aside as Beth and Finn both clambered out of their chairs, Finn with a lot of stumbling.

'I'm fine,' he reassured me. 'Don't worry, my room isn't far from here, anyway.'

'Do you know the way?' I asked. 'I don't want you to get lost because of the lights, or led astray by the doors.' Morgan looked up at me like I was crazy.

'What lights?'

Ah, yes. I had forgotten that the castle looked somewhat normal to guests. Morgan probably couldn't see the floating candles, or the spinning paintings. That was a blessing, at least.

'I will show him the way, don't worry,' said Beth. That wasn't reassuring at all.

I grabbed hold of Finn's arm.

'Look after Morgan tonight, please,' I asked him. Finn blinked up at me and held his arm up into a salute. I had to take that as a yes, because it was clear I wasn't going to get anything else.

'You can sleep in here, if you are nervous,' I whispered to Morgan.

Morgan rolled his eyes.

'I'm fine, Aunty H. I can look after myself, don't worry.' He pulled up his jumper sleave to show me a thick leather band around his wrist. Strapped to it were at least a dozen tiny vials, each a different colour.

I smiled proudly and waved him off, a little more at ease to see how prepared he was.

As they all began to amble downstairs, with Morgan practically carrying Finn, more strikes of lightning shot out around the tower. As the thunder crashed, I began wondering if it was really just me that was scared.

Chapter 16

The storm raged on into the night, the bright flashes of light and claps of thunder making it impossible for me to sleep. If I was going to stay in this tower, I would need to sort out some kind of screening for all of these windows. The view was beautiful, but there was nothing convenient about living in a glass dome.

I stood up on the bed and reached for the purple fabric that had been draped over the beams of the four-poster bed, but it was no good. They were decoration only and they slipped down as I tried to untangle them. I needed to get proper curtains up around this canopy.

I fell back down and sank into layers of bedsheets.

The bed was as soft as a cloud, but I missed my little bedroom back home, with my thin patchwork quilt, fluffy nightgown, and blackout blinds.

Was I ever going to sleep in my own bed again? My room at home was small and dusty and the floor creaked every time I moved. But it was *mine*.

I had half-made potions at home, and coven members that needed me. Would I ever be able to explain to them what happened?

I suddenly remembered the chat I had with Heston in this very room, when I had told him that I wanted to leave.

Things had been so hectic since then that I hadn't had a chance to think about it.

What had he said? That it would be hard for the house to let me go?

I jumped up out of the bed and went over to the bookshelf. A flash of light illuminated the room again and I spotted it, still lying on the floor as I had left it, its pages splayed out.

Had it been a coincidence? Or had Heston wanted me to read it?

I picked up the journal gently and carried it back to the bed.

I sent magic out to the candles, lighting the room with a flickering glow, and pulled the thick covers up over me. I blew on my hot chocolate and stirred it with a cinnamon stick. Then, settled finally, I began at the first page. It was headed with a neatly scrawled date, and just a name, Frankincense. H. Oaken.

Frankincense.

LIFE'S A WITCH

No, surely not?

I laughed aloud, but my voice was lost in the sound of the hammering rain and cracking thunder.

Frank was an odd enough name for an old wizard, but it was short for Frankincense!

I had a feeling this was going to be good. I read the first page, and flicked through the rest, stopping at important parts, and taking little notes as I went.

7.01.15

Well, that's it then. The new king William has been appointed and I am to be his Royal wizard! So much for all of my years of training, so much for all my damned plans!

Just more proof that this entire system is corrupt!

Fifty years I have apprenticed here under Doctor Knome.

Fifty years of promises and lies and hoping.

It is no secret that I wanted to be head pharmacist. It has been my lifelong goal and I have talked openly of it enough. That damned pharmacist is already 200 years old if he's a day! Why won't the wretched man retire?

I suppose I have brought this upon myself, for being naïve enough to believe that winning the games would guarantee me my place. Maybe this is punishment for my impatience.

Alas, in the end, I am undone, as I always am, by my own skills. Now I will be the plaything of the court, flitting about making foolish observations and prophecies to entertain them, when I should be doing proper magic, with no one but myself to account for!

Perhaps if I had waited it out for one more monarch to die before I made my move, then things would be different now, and I would still be toiling under Doctor Knome. The Royal wizard Mary would have some other fool as a replacement.

She only lasted one monarch, how ridiculous. She was an abysmal wizard, though, anyone could see that. Though, her predecessor was a pig, and I suppose it doesn't take much to be better than that. I curse the very day I helped that witch with her back ache. She must have had her eyes set on me from that very day, because the damned woman asked for me by name. Then the court decided it all without even asking me.

So Royal wizard it is.

~~Maybe when this monarch dies I can try again.~~

~~Is that Treasonous?~~

Oh well, here is an updated cookie recipe. I have omitted the dash of fairy dust, as it was just too lumpy:

½ cup of butter
¼ cup cream cheese
¾ cup brown sugar
¼ cup granulated sugar
1 egg
1 tsp vanilla essence
1 tsp essence of joy
2¼ cup flour
2 tsp corn starch

LIFE'S A WITCH

½ tsp salt
1 tsp baking soda
2 cups chocolate chips (a mix of milk and white is best)

I looked up from the pages for a moment. So Frank hadn't wanted to be a wizard, either? He was definitely skilful with magic, though, or else he wouldn't have all these potions and spell books.

I continued with the next dated entry in the journal.

09.01.15

I met the king today. He seemed much like his father, the frivolous and cold-blooded sort.

I had wanted his brother, Prince Trevor, to succeed personally, as I had met him many a time at the infirmary. However, the king won by popular vote and here we are.

The brother is to be sent away to the Court of Bone. Which is a shame, he seemed the more pleasant of the two.

This king has a grown-up son and heir already lined up, which I suppose swayed the vote.

The son is very sure of himself, and I did not care for him at all. He winked at me when we were introduced! A typical, sure-of-himself vampire.

Sometimes, I wonder what I am even doing in this court. I'm half elf, for goodness sake. I could be lauding it up in the Briar court right now if I so chose. Instead, here I am, creating potions so the heir can dye his hair green! What a waste of my talent.

No recipe today, even baking couldn't alleviate this foul mood.

15.01.15

Nothing of note. The magic I perform now is menial, what is even the point? The Royal Heir has invited me to dinner tonight, he tells me I entertain him.

Wonderful, exactly what I have strived for in this life. All that training, just so that an egotistical prince can humiliate me.

15.01.15

Dinner was nice, actually.

It was just us, in the Royal Library. The prince has some interest in food and astronomy and wanted to pick my brain. Well, those are two things we can talk about, I suppose.

A spiced cake was served as desert. I have attempted to guess the recipe from taste:

2¼ cups flour
1 tsp baking powder
1 tsp baking soda
½ tsp salt
2½ tsp cinnamon
1 tsp ground nutmeg
1 tsp ground ginger

LIFE'S A WITCH

½ tsp allspice
¼ tsp ground cloves
1¾ cup light-brown sugar
¾ cup oil
¾ cup applesauce
4 large eggs
2 tsp vanilla extract
1 cup buttermilk
1 cup chopped pecans

20.01.15

Bit drunk to be honest. Doctor Knome decided to die last evening. She didn't warn me, but her letter wished me well. She left me her cauldron.

20.02.15

There is a ball coming, to celebrate some charity that the king supports. I am to ascertain the correct date for it.

One good thing has come of this position, I have plenty of time alone to practise new spells and potions. The king rarely asks anything of me, and the court staff are too busy fighting among themselves for his favour, while trying to work out if our new king is kindly or cruel, wise or feckless. Either would be fine by them, of course. The role seems to have little to do with ruling, and much to do with throwing parties and appearing to be the very picture of what a vampire should be.

I suppose he and his son have that part down. I have yet to see him drink blood, though. Do vampires do that anymore?

21.02.15
I asked the prince and, apparently, vampires do drink blood, but it seems to be more for... fun. At least, he seemed to enjoy biting me. I suppose I set myself up for that.

Though... it wasn't completely unpleasant.

7.03.15
He wants his hair red now. I thought the black suited best, but he is stubborn.

8.07.15
I have not written much lately, I find I spend much time with Edward. He is interested in learning the craft, and as Royal wizard I suppose it is my job to teach him. He is quite smart though, I will admit.

16.09.15
Edward is to be sent away for a while, to visit his uncle in the Court of Bone.

He asked permission for me to accompany him. But the king has refused. As Royal wizard, I must stay. ~~*I am devastated*~~

03.01.17
Much has happened since I last wrote. There was a small altercation... well, a small war between the elves in the north and the vampires of the north.

LIFE'S A WITCH

As I am half elf. The king thought it best I be locked away, per chance that I might switch sides and spy.

The matter is settled now, however, and the king has reinstated me.

Edward is coming home from the Court of Bone, with a new bride, and a child.

I believe he has forgotten me.

The days are cold, my magic faulters lately.

15.01.17

The child has been presented at court. He is named Heston.

20.01.17

There is a strong outbreak of grime-flu, and the king's child is sick. The Royal pharmacy has been unable to help. It will not kill him, of course, but he is very sickly.

Edward has come to me to ask for a cure.

I am searching through my old books. If only Knome was here.

23.01.17

King William has died.

The Manor is in uproar.

Edward is king now, and Ann is queen.

26.01.17

Edward is suffering. His son is unwell, and his father is gone. There are rumours that he is the one who poisoned William, but I know that could not be the case. It takes more than a simple dose of poison to dispose of a vampire.

Those same gossips say that he is poisoning his own son. Who do they take Edward for? He isn't some power-mad brute.

His uncle has come to comfort him. At least, it is good to see Trevor again.

27.01.17

I have created a spectacular potion! It is truly my best work.

I based it on a potion of good health and longevity that dear old Knome had written down in her journals. I knew if I searched enough I would find something.

Perhaps I should start using my journals to write down more of my recipes...

Never mind, I can do that later.

I adapted Knome's potion, and now I know that little Heston will be well.

He is the most bonny thing.

26.01.17

It seems to have worked. Heston is well, and Edward is pleased. He took me aside and praised my skills, with tears in his eyes.

It felt like old times for a moment.

1.02.17

So the games have begun and the word is that a young witch from the city has come down to try for my job. Good luck to her, I say!

LIFE'S A WITCH

I never wanted this damn job to begin with.
And what has it brought me? A broken heart, years of wasted knowledge and a two-year stay in a prison cell. Perhaps I will even compete for Royal pharmacist again. ~~Or maybe I will just leave this place, go back home for a while.~~

02.02.17
Edward has asked me to be his Royal wizard.
I don't think I could say no... even if I wanted to.
But the games are tomorrow, and I haven't prepared.

03.02.17
I won. I was nervous, but now that it's over, I feel a little stupid. There was no real competition. News of my healing little Heston had spread and that convinced many competitors to back out, so my fate was already sealed. The young witch showed up, but had already backed out in heart, if not physically...

I didn't need to read any more. The answer had been staring me in the face this entire time.

The games.

Heston had asked me to be his Royal wizard, but if someone were to compete for that title in the games, then they would have a valid claim, and I could step down. Leaving me free to go back home!

~ 139 ~

Would Heston let me go back home, though? Or would he just appoint me to some other task? He had to know that it wasn't my fault his father died.

It couldn't have been my potion.

It was a hard task, but I could see the light at the end of the tunnel.

I needed to get someone to run against me as wizard, and I needed to find out exactly what killed King Edward. I had no idea where to start with the latter, but the former was obvious.

It was time to pay a little visit to Frankincense H. Oaken.

Chapter 17

I had planned this out to the most miniscule of details. Finn had found where the oubliette was located. We were going to go during the middle of the Eating games, when Heston would be occupied. I had three vials of sleeping gas tucked into my belt.

My athame was hidden under my sleeve for easy access and I had a memory spell revised to use on the guards. Spoken spells weren't really my forte, but I couldn't risk Morgan coming.

As it happened, the moment I got down into the dungeon all the attendants and guards broke out into a chorus of 'Make way for the Royal wizard.' They all bowed their heads and moved out of my way as though they had been expecting me.

It was a long, twisty corridor, and at every corner I was prepared for resistance. However, it was clear by the fifth or sixth 'Make way for the Royal wizard' that I had prepared for nothing. Maybe this gig had more authority than I had actually realised.

I reached the end of the corridor, where two guards stood at either side of a barricaded iron door. They nodded at my arrival and began pulling a thick, metal chain, which opened up the bars on the door. I hesitated a moment, wondering if this was all a trap and I was about to become the second Royal wizard to be locked inside the oubliette.

Better safe than sorry.

I threw the glass vial down onto the floor and stomped on it, crushing the glass into the stone and releasing the pink gas. It expanded and seeped into every inch of the room.

'That's very pretty,' said one of the guards. I heard him take in a long, deep breath through his nose.

'What does that smell remind you of, Roger?' he asked the other guard.

'Strawberries and ice cream, I think, Alfred,' the second guard replied.

'Oh, don't, you will make me hungry,' said Alfred. 'Still three hours before shift change.'

'You should have brought lunch,' scolded the guard named Roger. By this point, the gas had cleared and both guards were still standing happily at their post.

I watched them, dumbfounded. They should have passed out the moment they breathed in the potion. They stared back at me, expectantly.

LIFE'S A WITCH

The silence stretched on for a while as I waited for them to collapse. I knew the potion was perfect, for I had made it myself. So, why wasn't it working?

'Do you think that was supposed to do more than just smell nice?' Roger hissed to the other guard out the corner of his mouth.

'Probably,' whispered Alfred. 'Should we tell her that we can't be spelled?' They were literally standing three feet away from me, so even if they had been whispering quietly, I would have been able to hear.

'I think she has probably realised,' Roger answered.

'She looks a little disappointed. Should we play along?'

I rolled my eyes, hiked up my robe and walked past them, right into the oubliette. As I went, I heard Roger whisper.

'Thank the Dark Lord for that. It was getting a little awkward there.'

'Too true, Rog,' replied Alfred.

I gritted my teeth together and ignored them. I still wasn't completely sure what an oubliette was, but I certainly hadn't expected the heavy dungeon gates to give way onto a beautiful greenland.

Trees and plants grew wild from the forest floor. There was sunlight and the sound of crashing waves in the distance. This place had been created by magic. The trees were lush and bore every type of fruit and nut you could think of, while vines filled with strawberries and large, ripe tomatoes twisted up from the ground. There were logs overflowing with different types of fungus and mushroom. As I walked further into the woodland, I saw there were herb gardens of sage, dill, rosemary and mint. Colourful wild flowers bloomed up so high that I couldn't even see through them. I bent down and ran my fingers through a collection of green four-leaf clovers, dripping with sparkling morning dew.

This place was a witch's dream. The potions I could make here!

'It would appear that I have a visitor,' came a voice.

I clutched my chest in surprise as Frankincense stood from his hidden perch on a felled tree, just a few feet from me.

He had swapped his purple robes for forest green ones, which blended in perfectly with the surrounding greenery.

'Oh, hello,' I said, laughing shyly. 'I didn't see you there.'

The wizard's long, white hair was tied back with a ribbon, and looked just as luxurious as it had in the ballroom. I had an odd urge to reach out and touch it.

'Hello, witch of Broome,' he said.

I smiled sheepishly, a little unnerved by his use of my family name. As far as I could remember, I hadn't told him my first name.

'Hello, Frankincense,' I replied, trying to pull back some of the power. He didn't seem concerned that I knew his name, either, and sat back down on his log and pulled something onto his lap. It was a thick, brown, knitted blanket, and in his hands were a set of long knitting needles.

They continued to click away hurriedly, adding stitch after stitch to the blanket, even when he took his hands away. I watched for a moment, mesmerised.

'I am glad you have come,' the wizard said, snapping my attention away. 'I was anxious to meet my replacement.'

He patted the space next to him and I walked over, brushing through the tall, wild lavender that separated us. I couldn't bring myself to sit next to the wizard, though.

'So, why *have* you come?' he asked, staring up at me curiously.

I had fully prepared my speech in advance. I knew exactly how I was going to bring up the subject of the games. I opened my mouth with the *sole* intention of asking him to run against me, just as I had practised.

But instead, I asked him something so baffling, that even he looked surprised.

'Did you and the old king love one another, even to the end? Is that why he had no other children?'

The wizard's eyes widened slightly in surprise. He looked a little unnerved for a moment, then he broke out into a small smile and nodded.

'We did, and it is not why.'

'How did that work?' I asked. 'He was married, wasn't he? To Heston's mother?'

'There are many different ways to love,' the wizard began. 'Ann, Heston's mother, was a princess from the Court of Bone, and it was a love born only of duty. Yet, it flourished into friendship and warmth over time She was a wonderful woman.' Frank smiled fondly as he looked down at his work, his mind clearly in another time. 'Though we did not always get along in the beginning, I grew to be good friends with her.'

'What happened to her?' I asked, deciding to settle down on the damp log next to him.

He spread some of his blanket over my knees, and I accepted it thankfully.

We must have looked for all the world like a grandfather and granddaughter, sharing a tender moment.

'She left,' he said, sounding a little sad. 'Vampires are often restless creatures. They live a very long time, and having to stay put in one place for centuries can wear a bit on the soul.'

I nodded. I could resonate with the idea that there was something or someone out there waiting impatiently for you, while you dithered away the days.

'I suppose she will come back, some time,' he added. 'She loved Heston dearly, and I am sure she would like to see him now that he is king.'

'He didn't want to be king,' I said.

'Oh, I know,' said the wizard. 'He wants to have all the fun, without any of the obligation. I have watched that boy grow up and he never did know what was good for him.' He sounded like a parent, and I began to wonder how close his role to Heston had actually been.

LIFE'S A WITCH

'I'm sorry the old king is dead,' I said lamely. I wasn't sure if the wizard knew my part in it, but I couldn't bring myself to mention that now.

'Oh, I knew it was coming,' said Frankincense. 'We had spoken at length about the whole thing. He was ready to go.' A tear slipped down from his nose onto the yarn, despite his words. I didn't know what to say, so I patted his hand in what I hoped was a sympathetic way.

'Is that the reason you came to visit me?' he asked, brushing his eyes and clearing his throat.

'No,' I said, caught off guard. 'Well, yes. That and…' I trailed off.

'What is it?' he encouraged.

'Well, I feel guilty,' I admitted, saying yet another thing I hadn't planned to. 'I have usurped your entire life. All of your work is now sitting on shelves next to mine. I am using your potion mixes and recipes from your books. My cauldron smashed yours, the spiteful thing! And..' I hesitated, but he nodded for me to continue. 'I am reading your diaries and sleeping in your bed!'

The wizard laughed.

'So, you came here for my blessing?' he asked.

I shrugged, feeling uncomfortable.

'Witch of Broome Hill, there is nothing you, nor I, could do or say to fix what has happened.' He gave a low chuckle. 'I had no say in it back when I was appointed, and you have no say now. We are all at the changeable whim of the crown, as it has always been, and so it will continue to be.'

He didn't sound upset, though. He looked a little nostalgic, actually.

'Who am I to complain, though?' Frankincense continued. 'Dear Heston has built me my own personalised oubliette. And, after years of telling me to take it easy, he has forced me into a comfortable retirement. I have everything I could ever need here. Look around… what more could I ask for?'

I laughed nervously, not sure if his words were bitter or sincere. However, he certainly looked at ease in this magical forest-dungeon.

'No use in regretting the things we can't change,' he added, patting my knee reassuringly.

'Well… that's the thing,' I started, nervously. 'There is something we could do.' I sat up straighter and took hold of his hands.

'The winner of the mourning games gets to become a member of the king's staff! They can choose any placement that they want. So, if you win in the wizard and witchcraft games, you could be reinstated as Royal wizard and I could go home.' The wizard stared at me blankly, as if he was trying to take this in.

'Only a few weeks into retirement and someone is already trying to pull me out of it,' he grumbled.

LIFE'S A WITCH

For a moment, I felt my stomach drop, certain that he was going to refuse. But then he smiled and a sly gleam appeared in his warm, brown eyes.

'I had already thought this myself, I confess,' he replied. 'But I am imprisoned. And, as nice a prison as this is, it is still prison.'

'Let me sort that out,' I said confidently, with absolutely no idea how I would go about it. The wizard seemed to see right through me. However, he smiled and nodded all the same.

'Are you sure you want this, though?' I asked, concerned that I was somehow forcing him back into a role he had tired of.

'I think if there were no other reason, I would do it out of spite alone!' Frankincense laughed. 'However, being Royal wizard was more than a job for me – it was my life. I think that I have earned the right to decide when I leave it, don't you?'

I nodded. I think we both had a lot in common, actually.

Chapter 18

There was only one person who could free Frank, and that was Heston. I paced my tower room for many an hour after I got back from the oubliette, wondering if I should just ask him. He was the one who had shown me the book, after all. Therefore, he could probably ascertain where it would lead me.

There was still a lot of doubt in my mind. Maybe I was giving him too much credit and he had just been playing with that book randomly?

It didn't seem likely, though. As a witch, I didn't believe in coincidence, anyway.

No, I was sure Heston had meant for me to find that passage about the games. However, if he really wanted to help me, then surely Frank wouldn't still be locked up now?

It's always better to be safe than sorry, and I decided that a spell of obedience would be the best course of action.

LIFE'S A WITCH

The shelf life of obedience spells was notoriously short. The strongest one I had managed to make only lasted twenty-four hours, and the wizarding and witchcraft games were set for tomorrow.

If I planned this well, I would be able to get Frankincense out before the spell wore off.

'She's plotting something, don't you think?' I overheard Finn ask Morgan.

'Definitely,' Morgan answered. They were both sitting at the table, drinking tea and eating a batch of chocolate chip cookies that I had made earlier that day using one of the wizard's recipes. Beth was there, also, perched on the window seat, looking gloomily out at the city. Her hair was coloured black and green today, and she had added back lace to the cuff of her attendant's uniform. There was a hole in the fabric, through which her thumb was pushed through.

'I could be plotting things, if I was the queen,' she mumbled wretchedly. Finn rolled his eyes and Morgan snorted into his tea.

I stopped pacing and turned to them, my hands on my hips.

'Oh, I know that stance,' said Morgan. 'It means we are probably going to have to help.' Finn groaned at this suggestion and sank down in his chair.

'Yes, that's right,' I said as I rolled up my sleeves and pulled the Broome grimoire from its spot under the bed. It took a lot of effort, because the book was enormous. I carried it to the table and slammed it down, sending empty teacups rattling and rolling away.

I flicked through the pages until I found the spell I needed, then turned the book around so that Finn and Morgan could see it.

'You are going to make this potion up for me,' I said. Morgan's eyes lit up as he leant forward in his chair.

'This is a really advanced potion,' he said, whistling.

'I do not like the look of that,' Finn complained as he read the title.

'Oh, don't worry,' I replied. 'We won't use it on anyone. It's just to win the trials.'

'I really don't want to be a part of this,' Finn continued. 'This is treason.'

'Oh, stop worrying,' I scolded. 'It will be fine. Don't you trust me?' Finn shook his head.

'Morgan, you will need this.' I took my athame from my sleeve and handed it over to him, hilt first.

For a moment, he didn't take it, staring in awe at the black, emerald-encrusted dagger.

'Go on,' I urged. He looked unsure, but took it anyway. 'It was your grandfather's, so it's as much yours as it is mine,' I added. 'It should work, all the same.'

'Thank you,' he breathed.

'All the ingredients, bar one, should be on these shelves,' I said, indicating to the relevant shelves behind me. 'Make sure to measure and weigh out everything perfectly.'

LIFE'S A WITCH

Then, I turned the page to show them another recipe. 'This is the nullifying spell. You have to make that, too. Just in case.'

'And what are you going to be doing? While we make this treasonous spell?' Finn accused.

'I will be collecting the last ingredient for it, *and* putting the first half of our plan in motion.'

'I hate everything about this plan,' Finn complained. I ignored him.

Walking over to Morgan, I ruffled his hair. He was still staring at the athame in awe.

'Wait until you see Granny's dagger,' I said. 'That one is truly something to behold.'

'It can't pass to me, though,' replied Morgan. 'That one is only for the Broome women. This one…'

'Who says you can't have it!' I said. 'It's likely you will end up with them all, dear boy. Goddess knows you have the skill.' Morgan looked up at me self-consciously.

'I might not be as good as you all think,' he said.

'Nonsense! You are my nephew and I think you are amazing. You would be worthy of those daggers, even if you couldn't do a lick of magic.'

'Oh stop,' he said, embarrassed.

'I will, because you have a big spell to create, and I need to leave you to it,' I replied. Then I turned to Finn. 'Make sure you help him! I will be back soon.'

Finn mumbled something under his breath, but nodded all the same.

Just before I started my descent down the tower steps, I saw the fire in the hearth magically erupt into life.

You got this, kid.

When I got to bottom of the stairs, I was pleasantly surprised to see Posy, the doctor from the infirmary, at the other end of the corridor, on her way from one room to another.

I raced down to catch up with her. She was talking to an attendant and, as I got near, I realised they were sharing outfit ideas for the Pumpkin Ball.

'I'm going to be an actual pumpkin,' said the attendant. 'It's a spell, so anyone who looks at me will see a pumpkin.'

'That's… interesting,' said Posy, politely.

'Yeah, and then, later on in the night, the spell will fade to reveal a skin-tight orange gown,' continued the attendant. 'If that doesn't get the king's eye, then I don't know what will!'

'That will certainly be eye-catching…' agreed Posy.

The attendant interrupted hastily as she saw me approach.

'Good luck for tonight!' the attendant said. 'She then shot me a dirty look and hurried away down the hallway.

'Oh, she doesn't like me,' I said.

'Hello!' greeted Posy, looking genuinely happy to see me. 'Don't mind Kate,' she continued. 'She's just jealous of you.'

'Of me? Why?' I asked in surprise.

LIFE'S A WITCH

Posy looked at me as though I should know.

'Because, she has been Royal Library cleaner for three days now and the king hasn't looked at her once. But he looks at you.' I rolled my eyes and looked at my feet to try to hide the blush on my cheeks.

'Couldn't she be jealous of my powers, or something *actually* important?' I replied.

'Oh, that too, of course,' Posy said. 'But don't look down your nose at a girl who wants to impress a man in power,' she scolded, not unkindly. 'He's very handsome, and marrying him would mean becoming queen, and who wouldn't want that job?'

'I wouldn't,' I mumbled.

'What brings you this way, anyway?' Posy asked, changing the subject.

'I was on my way to see you, actually,' I admitted.

'Oh! What can I help you with?' she asked, looking pleasantly surprised.

I hesitated for a moment, not sure if I ought to involve Posy in this. What if something went wrong and it came back to her? What if she refused to help in the first place, and told someone what I was up to?

This was all foolish worrying, though. As the Royal wizard, making potions was literally what I was there for.

'I am looking for a few ingredients for a spell,' I said finally.

'Well, don't look so worried!' Posy said, reading the nervous look on my face. 'I can definitely help with that!' she laughed. 'We have all sorts of things stocked at the pharmacy. What are you after?'

'Nothing too rare,' I replied.

Posy led the way to the infirmary and then beyond into her office, where a couple of nurses were sitting around a large desk, playing a card game. The looked up in interest when we walked in.

'The pharmacists are pretty uptight about their stock, but this is *royal* business,' said Posy, as she pulled a large set of jangling keys from her lab coat pocket and began flicking through them. When she found the one she wanted, she waved the nurses out of her way and pressed some button or latch that was hidden under the office desk.

'Watch yourself, Posy!' complained one of the nurses as his cards fell to the floor. 'I was about to win!'

'Only because you are cheating, Mike,' mumbled the other.

At the press of the button, a panel at the back of the room slid open, revealing a hidden glass cabinet filled with a vast array of jars, boxes and parcels. Posy ran over and stuck the key into the lock. As she turned it, the glass doors swung open.

'What are you looking for?' she asked. 'This is just the stock for the infirmary. The actual pharmacy is near the gardens, so if it isn't here, we can go there.'

'Ugh, you don't want that,' said one of the nurses from his place at the table. 'The pharmacists are stuck-up toss—'

'Thank you, Greg,' said Posy, silencing him. 'Go check on bed three, won't you?'

'I need distilled sunlight,' I said, as I shifted through the large bottles of knotweed, bat drool, firewart and knapped flint.

'Oh, is this it?' asked Posy, pulling out a miniscule jar of black liquid from towards the back. 'Oh, no, distilled terror,' she said, hastily putting it back.

We both sifted through the jars for a while until, eventually, I found it. A bright white liquid, in a small test tube. I went to reach for it, but Posy quickly grabbed it before I could.

She wiggled her finger at me. 'You can have this,' she said. 'But, it comes at a price.'

'Ok…' I said, feeling apprehensive.

'You have to let me pick out your robes for the Pumpkin Ball!' she said excitedly.

I laughed nervously, and breathed a sigh of relief.

'You don't have to look so worried all the time,' Posy said, sincerely. 'I am just trying to be your friend.' She rolled the test tube in her hand and looked down at it absently for a moment.

'I actually grew up around humans, away from the magical world,' she admitted, 'and I have always felt like a bit of an outcast here. I like superhero movies, and pumpkin spice latte, and the Great British Bake-off. It would be brill if I could talk to someone who at least *knows* what those things are.'

'I like those things, too,' I said. 'Well, not bake-offs. I'm more of a MasterChef girl, but I will happily chat with you about it,' I said, sincerely.

Posy handed over the tube and I pocketed it.

'It's a deal, then,' she said.

Chapter 19

I found Heston in his library, standing by the bay window, poring over a book with a teacup balanced delicately in his hands. He looked up when I entered. My heart juddered uncomfortably in my chest as I met his eyes.

Why did he have this power to make me so nervous!

'Hodge, to what do I owe this pleasure?' he asked as he placed the book down.

'I was looking to do some research,' I lied, 'about astronomy.'

He stared at me steadily for a moment, as if he could see right through my lie and was deciding whether or not to call it out. Then, wordlessly, he made his way over to the spiral staircase.

I watched him as he climbed up to the balcony. He searched the shelves there for a bit, before leaning over the banister and waving a book at me.

'Here,' he said, as he threw down a small, red, fabric-bound book.

I darted forwards and managed to catch it clumsily before it hit the hard floor.

I flipped it in my hands. 'Stars and Planets for the Young Novice.'

I rolled my eyes, but plastered a smile on my face as he came back down the steps and approached me, the corners of his mouth turned up in a small smirk.

'That should explain everything you need,' he said.

'Thanks,' I smiled, uneasily. I felt a bit at a loss. I had planned to invite him out for a drink, but my gaze strayed to the teapot already steaming by the window.

'Would you like a cup?' he asked, noticing my stare. I nodded, not trusting my words.

He gestured for me to sit at the window and went to pour the tea into a cup. I took the pot from his hands clumsily.

'I… I'll do it!' I said.

'You're so nervous. Do you want to talk about it?' he asked, softly. 'I don't want you to be on edge with me, Hodge.'

I felt more guilty than ever now, not expecting him to have any compassion regarding the effect his behaviour had on me. But how could I tell him that I was nervous about something entirely different now?

I shook my head and attempted a smile. I had fully prepared to accidently spill his cup. However, I didn't have to, as it was already empty. I waited a moment for him to look away, and praised the goddess when he did just that, walking over to grab a blanket from the armchair near the fireplace. I quickly slipped the potion of obedience into his cup before he turned back and handed the blanket over to me.

'You are shaking,' he said. 'Are you cold?'

'A little,' I lied again.

He placed the blanket over my shoulders and accepted the cup when I handed it to him.

'Hodge,' he said, his voice serious. 'Can we talk about what happened yesterday?'

'Let's just forget it,' I said, with a forced laugh. 'We're both adults, these things happen.'

He frowned and sat next to me, holding the cup in both hands.

'I don't want to forget it,' he breathed. 'I want to repeat it. I want to spend more time with you, and get to know you.'

'Not much to know,' I laughed. I didn't need this now. I couldn't listen to this handsome king try to confess that he had feelings for me, not when I was literally trying to bespell him to my will. It was too much.

'Hodge, let me put you out of your misery,' he said. 'Whatever you are trying to poison me with, it won't work.' He drained the entire teacup of potion in one go and slammed it down on the seat next to me, before gathering my hands in his.

'This is important,' he began. 'From the moment I met you, I have felt drawn to you, and I know you feel the same.'

I couldn't take in his words. I stared down at the empty teacup, my heart pounding.

'You knew?' I asked.

'Knew what?' he snapped, clearly frustrated by me.

'That I was trying to spell you.'

'You were fairly obvious, Hodge,' he sighed. It was the kind of sigh specifically set aside for naughty children – frustrated, but tender. 'I'm starting to think you don't poison people very often.'

'Of course I don't,' I said.

'So, why did you try to poison me?'

'Well, give it a moment first, to see if it works.'

'What kind of poison was it?' he asked. I wished he would stop smiling at me like that. I would have preferred him to be angry.

'It's not poison at all. Stop saying that,' I snapped. He stared at me patiently, waiting for me to tell him everything. I wanted to lie, but then there was no point in that anymore.

'A spell of obedience.' After I had said it, I wished I could take it back. He genuinely looked surprised for a moment.

'Obedience?' he repeated. 'That is unexpected.' He stood up and paced a little, running his hands through his hair distractedly.

'You wanted me to do something?' he asked, looking me dead in the eyes. 'And you decided to spell me, when you could have just asked?'

I jumped up, spilling my tea on the floor and soaking the rug with black liquid. I hastily grabbed the cloth that had been wrapped around the hot teapot handle and wiped the tea off the carpet apologetically. Heston watched all of this, silently, his face devoid of all emotion.

'Look, I know it sounds bad,' I said, standing up and abandoning the spilled tea. 'But it wouldn't have hurt you.'

He stepped closer then, wordlessly, his face still a mask of calm. My heart began to race. I stepped back, but my heel hit the wall behind me. He had somehow walked me into a corner. He placed his hands either side of my head, resting them on the wall. I had nowhere to look but at him.

'It has hurt me,' he breathed. 'It has hurt me that you didn't feel you could come to me and ask.'

'Why would I do that?' I said. 'When it's you that has me trapped here.'

'I did not trap you here, Hodge.' He said each word slowly and darkly, his eyes staring into mine, occasionally slipping down to my lips. I licked them, self-consciously. 'You were the one who made a bargain with a vampire. You were the one that touched the stone phoenix, becoming the wizard and sealing your own fate,' he said through gritted teeth. I could see a tick in his tight jaw.

'I gave you the journal to help you,' he continued. 'When have I ever given you the impression that I wouldn't help you?'

His eyes searched mine and I looked down to the ground, unable to meet his direct gaze.

Roughly, he gripped the tip of my chin in his hand and pulled my head up to face him again.

'I hate it when you won't look at me,' he whispered. 'Am I that unattractive to you?' I almost laughed at the absurdity of that question, but the laugh died in my throat as he watched me with his stony gaze.

'What were those words again?' he continued. 'The ones you first used to describe me?' He looked away, darkly. 'Spiderlike. Creature.'

I remembered that.

But I hadn't meant those words grotesquely! Even before I knew his character, I hadn't thought he looked foul. Just… otherworldly. Not human.

Surely, he must have known how my traitorous thoughts had betrayed me?

But, of course he hadn't. I had hung the spell of fortitude around my neck from the day I arrived here. He wouldn't have been able to hear a single thought since then! Thank the goddess.

'Never mind,' he said, pushing away from the wall and walking back over to the bay window, turning his back to me.

LIFE'S A WITCH

I stared at his silhouette, framed against the large window, and it hit me again how striking he was. Tall, with long, graceful limbs, and an aura about him that made the air around him still. His sleek black hair was tied back with a patterned crimson ribbon, and I had to fight the urge to walk over and pull it free.

'How did you resist my spell?' I asked. 'You said the love potion took, so how did you resist this one?'

He turned and pulled a pendant from around his neck. It was a small circle of glass, about the size of a coin.

'I confess,' he said darkly. 'I am immune to many things, but not you, apparently.' I stepped over and took the glass in my hands, flipping it over to examine it. Magic radiated from the warm necklace. I looked up at him, confused.

'This is my magic,' I said. 'But I didn't make this.'

'No,' he admitted. 'That day at your shop, when I came to collect you, I stole some of your magic. My Royal pharmacist created a resistance spell from it.'

I thought back to that day, but I couldn't remember him doing anything other than sitting at the table before he took me away.

'You think a vampire prince would be so rude as to put his feet up on a witch's table for no good reason? At her covenstead, of all places?' He clicked his tongue in reproach.

'You were collecting my dust,' I guessed. 'From your boots?'

'I was collecting your dust,' he confirmed. 'I've never known anything like it. What is it made from? My guess is the remnants of past spells, built up over centuries?'

'Something like that, yes.'

We were silent then. I stood in his shadow, holding tight to the pendant, and him staring down at me. I felt afraid to move, afraid of what he would do.

Afraid of what I would do.

Eventually, he took my hands in his and pulled them away from the pendant, letting it drop back around his neck.

He pushed me away, ever so slightly, and let go of my hands.

'The wizard can come and go as he pleases,' Heston said, quietly. 'The guards have already been given the order. So go fetch him.'

I stared up at him in thanks, but he wouldn't meet my eyes.

'Hurry now, Royal witch. The games end tomorrow.'

Chapter 20

I walked for a long time after I left the library, feeling mentally exhausted. More than once, I stopped dead in my tracks and turned around to go back, before thinking better of it.

What would it achieve? I wasn't going to give in and start a romance with the vampire king.

I had spent most of my life giving in to other people and making hard choices.

I could make this one.

In stark contrast to my mood, the corridor seemed to be having some kind of disco around me, playing cheerful pipe music, with strobing purple lights flashing happily across the ceiling. At one point, streamers exploded overhead, floating down into my hair.

'Oh, piss off!' I yelled, angrily.

The corridor immediately plunged into pure darkness and I could no longer see my way ahead. I growled and kicked out at the thin air in frustration.

However, my leg connected with something hard and I gasped as a loud groan was followed quickly by a thump as someone, or something, fell to the floor. I was pretty sure that I had just kicked some unsuspecting attendant in the crotch.

I apologised profusely while I made a hasty exit, holding onto the wall for guidance and feeling very thankful that they couldn't see who I was.

'Can you turn on the lights, please?' I asked when I felt I had escaped to a safe enough distance. Nothing happened.

'Turn on the light!' I barked, remembering that this Manor had an aversion to courtesy.

The lights went on immediately, filling the corridor with a warm glow, all the better for me to see none other than Uncle Trevor sitting on the floor in front of me, with his knees drawn up in pain.

'Uh, did I do that?' I asked him, looking behind me, trying to figure out how I had got back here.

'Yes. This corridor loops around,' Trevor replied with a grimace.

Oh.

Awkward.

'Can you help me up?' he asked. I ran over and helped pull the vampire to a standing position.

LIFE'S A WITCH

'I really didn't do that on purpose,' I explained. 'I was just lost, and annoyed.'

'It's alright, no harm done,' he said, as he brushed himself down and took a steadying hold on my arm. 'I was on my way to the knife games,' he continued. 'Is that where you were headed?'

I opened my mouth to say no, but then I remembered that Posy had asked me to be there. I felt a stab of guilt, as she had been so helpful before.

I could always go and fetch the wizard later.

Just then, an attendant hurried past and I got an idea. I waved her down.

'Can you take a message to my nephew, please?' I asked her.

'I am a Royal baker…' she began to protest.

'Can I employ you as a Royal messenger for just a few moments?'

The attendant looked between me and Trevor, unsure.

'I'm sure that can be done,' Trevor said kindly. There always seemed to be an unspoken threat under the surface when Trevor spoke, and clearly the attendant thought so to, because her face paled slightly.

'I can do that,' she agreed. Obviously, she was just keen to be gone.

I scribbled a note down on a piece of paper that I found in my pocket and handed it over.

SIMONE NATALIE

Morgan,

Fetch Frank from the oubliette, Finn knows the way.

You don't need any spells to get through, but if you want you could take a sandwich for the guards. I think they would appreciate it.

Aunty H.

'He should be in the tower,' I said, as the attendant rolled the paper up and placed it inside her jacket.

I saw the attendant's face turn from white to green at the mention of the tower steps, and I felt guilty all over again. However, she hurried off, nonetheless.

'Ready?' Trevor asked. I nodded and he placed my hand in his, once again, as we headed off toward the throne room. It was an awkward walk, with neither of us saying a word. I tried to think of conversation starters, but the only thing I could think about was how I had managed to knee him in the privates twice now.

I was thankful when we reached the throne room. I could hear a loud jeering from the crowd inside, so the game must have already started. The guards opened the doors for us and the roar of the crowd reached ear-splitting heights.

I could see the top of Posy's sleek black hair and realised she was already in the ring. I broke away from Trevor, with a hurried apology, and pushed through the crowd to the front.

LIFE'S A WITCH

I got there just as Posy threw a needle-thin blade straight at the face of her opponent. I cried out in surprise and covered my eyes with my hands.

The crowd cheered excitedly and I could only guess that the blade had hit its mark.

I hesitated a moment, not sure of the sight I would be faced with when I uncovered my eyes.

However, just then, two small hands prised mine away from my face, and Posy was there, laughing heartily.

'Hedgehog, what are you doing?' she asked.

'Cowering in fear?' I suggested. Posy laughed and pointed towards her opponent. Reluctantly, I looked ahead, to see that the man had been impaled by the blade, right through his left earlobe.

A couple of attendants were attempting to pull it out, but having no luck at all. The man himself was staring at Posy with what could only be described as a look of love. She blew him a kiss and he pretended to catch it.

'Surely, there is no beating that?' Posy cried out. The crowd went wild at this.

'What do you think?' she asked me.

'That is very impressive,' I said in awe. 'How did you learn to do that?'

Posy shrugged. 'I used to be on the fencing team at high school.'

'What kind of high school did you go to?'

'A normal one, silly!' she laughed again.

The crowd settled as a loud, slow clapping filled the room. Heston stepped down from the dais and walked towards us.

Had he come here directly from the library?

He didn't meet my eye as he approached, staring instead at Posy.

'Well done, Doctor…' he praised. 'That was the most remarkable demonstration of swordsmanship. Are you sure you won't join my rank of elite assassins?' He held out a red ribbon with a gold medal attached.

Was that a joke, or did he actually have assassins working for him? That seemed a little illegal. Then again, Heston didn't seem the type to let something like that get in the way of what he wanted.

Posy bowed, her face alight with pride as she accepted the gold medal around her neck. She kissed it and held it up into the air. Her delight was catching and I found myself cheering along with the crowd.

'Doctor, you have shown yourself to be more worthy and more talented than any in your class,' continued Heston. 'As your reward, you may request a place in my household.' He reeled the speech off in a way that suggested he had repeated the same phrase many times before, and at this point he probably had.

Posy giggled, heady with the excitement of her success.

'Thank you, my King,' she replied, trying and failing to hide her smile and look solemn. She went down onto one knee at his feet. 'I am honoured by this opportunity, and humbly request to be the Royal physician.'

'Royal physician is a role not to be taken lightly,' Heston said gravely, as he looked down at Posy. 'If I accept your request, you will be responsible for the health of the Royal family, including myself and any heirs that I may have. It is not a job simply for accolade, but one of continuous learning and excessive patience. Do you feel ready to accept this role?'

'I do,' Posy answered without hesitation. Heston motioned for her to rise, and an attendant handed her paperwork to sign.

'As do I,' he agreed. 'I have spoken with the Royal pharmacist, and the current Royal physician. Both are happy for you to take over the role. Congratulations.'

Posy signed her name on the dotted line without any hesitation and squealed loudly. She turned to me and pulled me into a tight hug.

'I've done it!' she cried and bounced up in elation. I bounced along with her!

'Congratulations, Posy!' I said, genuinely pleased for her.

The music started up then and Posy pulled me onto the dance floor. As the winner, it was her responsibility to open up the dancing, so no one stopped her. She took hold of my forearms and I took hold of hers, and we spun and hopped clumsily along to the music. It felt amazing to dance with someone who seemed just as clueless as me.

'I can't believe I won,' she said, her face glowing with pride.

'Really? You seemed so confident before,' I replied. Posy scoffed loudly and grabbed a drink from the tray of a passing attendant. She chugged it down in one go.

'I was faking it until I made it!' she admitted. 'My mum's human, and I never met my vampire dad. The only reason I came to the Manor was because I needed to get my doctorate, and I heard it was easier here!'

'Was it?' I asked, trying desperately not to fall as we began to spin round and round in awkward ovals.

'Fuck off was it!' she cried loudly. A few people near us cheered, and raised their glasses at her words.

'But it doesn't matter,' she continued. 'I wouldn't want to be anywhere else. And now I am the youngest Royal physician, ever!'

'I'm so happy for you,' I said, truthfully.

'Thanks, Hedgehog.'

As we danced, my gaze kept wandering over to the dais, where Heston was deep in conversation with a beautiful vampire. She was dressed in a form-fitting silver gown and her long, blonde hair was secured with two ruby red daggers, a colour quite similar to Heston's eyes. As they spoke, she reached out a slender hand and touched him on his arm. I felt an uncomfortable stab of jealousy in my chest.

Would he ask her to dance?

LIFE'S A WITCH

I caught a glimpse of Uncle Trevor then, out of the corner of my eye, from the other side of the dais. He had just accepted a drink from an attendant and was now walking up the dais towards the chatty pair. I watched as he waved his hand over the glass and sprinkled something dark into the liquid. He twirled it with a roll of his wrist and smelt it, before approaching Heston.

I watched in trepidation as they exchanged a few short words, and Heston accepted the glass.

Panic fell over me in a sudden wave.

What had Uncle Trevor put in that drink?

Surely it couldn't have been... poison?

I had jumped to conclusions before, but I knew what I had seen this time. He had definitely mixed something into that drink!

I stopped dancing and pulled away from Posy.

'You okay?' she asked, concerned. I pushed my way through the dancers, forcing couples to separate and dodge out of my way.

'Don't drink it!' I screamed, as I sprinted up the dais steps and slapped the drink out of Heston's hand. It crashed to the marble floor. The glass shattered and spewed the shimmering pink concoction within all over the white marble floor. People around me gasped, and then fell into a stunned, suspenseful silence.

'So, was there a reason for that?' asked Heston, conversationally. His hand was suspended in mid-air, as if he was still holding the glass.

'Yes, he poisoned it!' I gasped, slightly out of breath from the run. I pointed an accusatory finger at Trevor, as adrenaline pumped through my veins. 'I saw him.'

Heston looked to his uncle for an explanation. 'Well, did you?' he prompted.

'Of course not,' said Trevor, who looked completely bewildered by my sudden outburst.

'I saw you put something into it!' I yelled. I could feel my face burn with frustration.

'Is that true, Uncle?' Heston pressed. 'Did you put something in my drink?'

'Well, yes I did, dear nephew,' Trevor admitted calmly.

'Hah! I knew it,' I cried triumphantly.

'Not poison… it was meant to be a surprise,' continued Trevor.

Wait… what? A deadly surprise?

Trevor tinkered with his robe pocket, then pulled out a small wooden box. He unclasped it and showed Heston the contents. I strained my neck to see, but couldn't get a good look.

'Oh,' sighed Heston, as he eyed the box. He looked pleased and I was beginning to suspect I had, once again, completely misread the situation.

'I gathered them myself, dear nephew,' continued Trevor. 'I knew you had not been able to make the journey back to the Court of Bone in a while, so I hoped to surprise you.'

'What is it?' I asked, as Heston took the box in his hands.

'It's cinnamon,' he explained, as he held the box out for me to inspect. 'My mother, the queen consort, planted the tree many years ago, at her ancestral home. It has a unique flavour that always reminds me of her.'

He took the box back and shut it. He looked up at his uncle, his face softened by a small, thankful smile.

'A truly appreciated gift, Uncle,' he said. He stood with his arms outstretched and the two vampires embraced one another.

The guests, who had been watching the exchange, cheered heartily. A few attendants came and cleaned up the mess that the shattered glass had produced, shooting me appalling looks as they did so, as loudly and as slowly as they possibly could. It was really awkward, actually.

Trevor turned to me then. 'You should be very proud of your Royal witch, though, Heston. She was wrong this time, but I believe it would be almost impossible for you to come to harm under her watch.'

Heston looked at me proudly and I felt my face blush.

'*Almost.*'

I looked up and met Trevor's eyes in surprise. Outwardly, he looked normal, but I was sure I was the only one to have heard the word aloud. No one else seemed to have noticed, or reacted to it.

Maybe I needed to get more sleep.

Chapter 21

I partied with Posy for hours, and only managed to sneak away when she and the competitor she had won against started playing a new kind of game, one played with tongues instead of swords.

Heston had disappeared early in the night. A ridiculous part of me had worried that he left with someone. However, I spotted the blonde-haired vampire dancing with someone else, so I pushed it to the back of my mind.

As I walked, I found myself near the Royal Library. I had to turn around completely, as I didn't trust myself to behave rationally if he was in there.

I practically ran the rest of the way to the tower steps.

Halfway up the stairs, I could hear the sound of raised voices.

In a panic, I dashed up the last few steps, my mind spinning in panic about what it could be. Thankfully, when I crossed the threshold, passed Nixie and into the dome tower room, I found Finn and Morgan laughing hysterically, while Beth was scolding them both about something.

'What's going on?' I asked, breathlessly. Finn was rolling on the floor, clutching his sides, and Morgan was sitting on the edge of my bed, tears of laughter running down his red face.

Then I saw it.

Frank was standing near the fireplace, looking very put upon. His floor-length locks of hair had been backcombed into an emo swoop. No longer silky white, his hair was a striped mix of black, purple and pink. His floor-length beard was dyed to match.

I stared in utter shock for a few moments, taking it all in.

'Why?' was all I could say. This set Finn and Morgan off again, laughing until they could hardly breathe.

'He drank my hair potion,' explained Beth. 'I suppose he thought it was his own. Personally, I think it looks good.'

'What… what was your hair potion doing here?' I asked, astounded. 'And why would he confuse it with his own?'

'I just made a new batch!' she cried. 'Your cauldron is bigger than mine!'

'You made that in *my* cauldron?'

LIFE'S A WITCH

'I want to know where *my* cauldron is,' Frank piped up. I looked at the wizard, then had to look away again for fear of laughing in his face.

'I told you, it was crushed,' I explained apologetically.

'I didn't realise you meant that literally,' he said, deadpan.

I held it together as long as I could, but the sheer spectacle of the stern, wrinkled wizard with a swoopy fringe was too much. I bent over, laughing and spluttering.

Beth cleared her throat angrily and stormed out of the tower room, having clearly had enough of the lot of us.

When I had calmed down enough, I went to sit with Morgan.

'So,' I asked, 'did you manage to create the spell I asked for?'

'I did,' he said proudly.

'Stunning bit of magic, that!' boomed Frank, having overheard us. 'I am very impressed, young man.' Morgan blushed a fierce red all the way to the tips of his ears, and I wondered if my blush was as obvious as his.

'It just needs the last ingredient, then,' I said, pulling from my robe the test tube that Posy had given me earlier. I handed it to Morgan.

He pulled a large jar from a pouch tied at his hip. He took it over to the table and carefully twisted open the cork seal. He did the same with the test tube and, very slowly, he transferred the contents into the jar. He then pushed in a new cork and sealed it with a heavy layer of red wax that he had left bubbling over the fireplace.

He shook the jar to combine the mixture properly. Lastly, he took the athame and waved it over the jar.

'Bloody work, will you,' he demanded.

I snorted loudly through my nose and Finn, who had been watching the whole thing very solemnly, broke out in a shocked laugh.

'Are those the magic words?' he asked.

'The words don't really mean anything,' explained Morgan. 'It's the intent behind them that binds the spell to work a certain way.'

Finn looked at me for confirmation and I nodded.

'It's true, little fairy,' said Frank. 'Magic is a chaotic and unstable thing. You can do everything right, follow a recipe exactly to the mark, but if the intent and force of will isn't there, then it won't work.'

He took the jar from Morgan's hand and examined it.

'I think you have it just right, boy,' he said. 'But what is the call for a potion like this? It's rare, and very specific.' Frank looked up at me. 'I won't let you use it, you know.'

I nodded. 'It's for the wizardry and witchcraft games tomorrow,' I explained. 'You are going to win with this potion.'

Frank looked at me, shocked for a moment, then he went back to examining the bottle.

LIFE'S A WITCH

'I suppose that's quite fitting, really,' he conceded. 'I won my last games with a cure fit for a vampire.'

'And you will win this one with a poison that could kill one,' I said.

'It's a bit potent,' he replied, sounding a little unsure.

'That's why you are going to use it on a blade,' I explained. 'No one would dare to test out a spell like this, so no one could possibly win against it.'

'That's a little clever, Broome witch,' said Frank, eyeing me over the bottle.

Chapter 22

That night, after everyone had gone to bed, I spent a long time reading through Frank's diaries.

He stopped writing about his personal life as the years went on, and filled the books with recipes for cakes, spells, potions, cheeses and even instructions on how to grow certain plants. He seemed to be always learning new things, gaining new skills, and it was clear he was the sort of person who strived to continue growing, no matter how old he got.

I envied him a bit, his ability to take a life that he hadn't planned for himself, and still find a huge sense of self and personal accomplishment.

It was also clear that he cared very much for Heston. He made notes of Heston's milestones throughout his childhood. From first words, to height, and favourite meals. I fell asleep with the book still clutched tightly in my hand.

It was touching to read.

LIFE'S A WITCH

The next day, I awoke with bright sunlight streaming through the window, to find Heston sitting at my bedside.

I jumped up, pulling the blankets over my pink, rainbow-covered pyjamas. I tried to smooth my hair down, but there was no containing it this early in the morning.

'What are you doing?' I demanded.

'You have a visitor this morning,' he replied. 'I didn't want you getting all in a flap like you did when Morgan arrived, so I decided I would come tell you myself. The phoenix let me in, so I presumed you were awake.'

'How long have you been here?' I snapped.

'I admire your hair,' he said, ignoring the question and reaching a hand out to touch the messy tangles. 'It's beautiful. I thought so when I first saw you, in the shoppe. You had a toy bat tangled in it, and I know you had no idea. It was very endearing.'

'Heston,' I warned. He smiled at me, almost sadly.

'It is the end of the games today, and I have a feeling I will be seeing much less of you in future,' he said. 'So forgive me my nostalgia.'

'Who is here?' I demanded, trying to get the conversation back on track.

'Your sister, Raven.'

I stared at him for a moment, astonished and unsure if I had misheard.

'Raven?' I asked. The vampire nodded.

'Raven came to the Manor?'

'Is that so strange?' he asked. 'When her sister and child are already here?'

'Raven hates magic,' I explained. 'She won't even go into the shoppe, so she would never willingly come to a place like this.'

'Well, I would guess that her love for you and Morgan is stronger than her hatred of my home,' said Heston. 'After all, your love of Morgan was stronger than your want for freedom.'

My mouth dropped open. 'I don't know what you mean,' I said, feigning ignorance. Heston laughed.

'Morgan sold the love potion, not you,' Heston said, simply. 'You are one of the dizziest witches I have ever met, Hodge. But, even you must remember that mind reading is a common vampire ability, or else what is this little trinket for?'

He held up his hand and dangling between his fingers was my hex bag. He must have taken it from around my neck while I slept. He opened his fist slightly and his glass pendant tumbled out to dangle next to my bag.

I stared a while before meeting his gaze, my heart beginning to flutter with trepidation.

Heston placed both items down on the bedside table and crossed one leg over the other.

'So, you see, we are both of us vulnerable,' he said, his voice a low whisper. 'Shall we talk now?'

LIFE'S A WITCH

'No, I need to see Raven,' I replied, attempting to climb up out of the bed. He stopped me with an outstretched hand. He tilted his head up to look at me, his face expressionless. Then, he nodded his head, indicating for me to sit down.

'Raven, Morgan, Frank, Beth and Finn are all in my library together. They can wait a few more moments.'

I nodded and sat back down on the bed.

'If you want me to let this go, then I will,' Heston said. I didn't need to ask what he meant by 'this', for he was obviously talking about the strange attraction we shared.

'I think you should,' I said. Heston met my eyes and I felt my face blush. It burnt more furiously when I remembered he would be able to read my thoughts now, and probably knew exactly how attractive I found him.

'If you could read *my* mind, then you would know the feeling is mutual, Hodge.' He uncrossed his legs and leant forward in his chair, looking at me intensely.

'I would like to offer you a place in my Manor,' he said with a sigh. I stared at him, caught off guard.

'You are free to come and go as you please,' he continued. 'No tricks, and no contract, if that's what you want.'

'What place?' I found myself asking.

'As a consulting witch. I would call on you, when I need your help or expertise. I still need to figure out what happened to my father, you could help with that? In the meantime, you can work at your shoppe, or travel, or whatever you wish to do. The choice is yours.'

What choice. It was back to the shoppe after this, back to the coven and the meetings – presuming Frank managed to win the games.

'You *do* have a choice, Hodge,' Heston said quietly. 'You had a choice when you took the shoppe, too. You made the choice to do what you felt was right.'

He was right, of course. I could have abandoned the coven to its own devices, left like Raven did and washed my hands of it. The coven was Granny's responsibility back then, not mine, and she left it easily enough. Why did I feel such a strong sense of duty towards it?

'Because that's who you are,' Heston said, listening to my thoughts.

'I need time to think about your offer,' I said.

'Yes, take your time. I'm not going anywhere,' he replied, leaning back. 'And… take your time to think over us, too. Because it doesn't have to be that serious, Hodge.'

I bit my lip, thinking about Frank's diary.

'I'm guessing you will need to marry someone at some point,' I said slowly, 'and that someone will probably be an influential vampire. Am I right?'

Heston gave a miniscule nod.

'Then, I don't see the point,' I admitted.

'Does there have to be a point?' he asked. 'Some things can just be done for the fun of it.'

'I don't think it would be fun,' I said coldly. 'I think it would be messy, and emotional and difficult.'

LIFE'S A WITCH

'All of life is those things, you can't hide away from it,' Heston replied, as he ran a frustrated hand through his hair, then looked straight at me. I refused to budge, though. After a while, he sighed and handed me back my hex bag from the table.

'Fine, Hodge,' he conceded. 'But think about my offer, will you?'

I nodded and placed the spell around my neck.

'I had a dress made for you, for the Pumpkin Ball tonight,' he said as he stood up. He indicated a large black box that was placed on the table.

'You can wear whatever you like, but I thought it would suit you.'

I nodded.

'Save me a dance?' he asked.

'As long as you promise not to spin me too fast,' I replied, with a small smile.

'I swear,' he whispered.

I looked up and met his eyes. He took a half step forward, and I wondered if he was thinking about the kiss we had shared. However, he seemed to catch himself. Turning away, he retreated down the tower steps without another word.

***

When I walked into the library, I had to do a double take.

Raven was sitting in the bay window, a cup of tea resting in her lap, her dark brown hair tied back from her beaming face. She wore a long black robe, one I hadn't seen in years that our mother used to wear, decorated with crescent moons.

She looked completely at ease. In fact, she looked better than I had seen her look in years.

At her feet was Morgan, legs crossed with a broadsword placed over them. Frank, still emo-fied, was standing nearby, and Finn and Beth were both lounging comfortably in the armchairs by the fire. They all looked at ease.

I walked into the room and Raven saw me first. She jumped up and ran over to me, tears in her pale blue eyes. She pulled me into a tight hug and I inhaled her familiar smell of grapefruit soap and sage.

'Raven, what are you doing her?' I spluttered out. 'What are you wearing?'

'Oh, H. It's been a crazy week,' she laughed, showing off her cheek dimples.

'You're telling me,' I replied. She took my hand and, together, we walked back to the window.

'When Morgan came and got me last week, I knew something bad had happened,' Raven explained. 'By the time I got to the shoppe, Bell was jangling like crazy.' Her words were all coming out in a rush. 'I couldn't find you anywhere, so I had to scry. I didn't think I could, because of the binding spell. But it worked and it felt so natural. The moment I stepped into the circle, I felt a kind of peace and familiarity that I hadn't felt in years.' She smiled.

I couldn't believe what I was hearing.

'There was something about being in the shoppe again,' she continued. 'It felt like coming home, H. It felt like a part of my heart had been missing, and I didn't even realise it until I walked back through those doors.'

Raven paused to look at me for a moment. 'I was so worried about you, that I called a circle meeting so that we could all send you healing vibes, and keep an eye on Morgan.'

'Did you run it?' I asked, shocked.

She broke into a beaming smile. The dimples on either side of her cheek popped, and she looked so young and full of life for a moment.

'I did,' she replied. 'And it was like second nature to me, H. I don't think I can go back to being mundane again.'

'I'm speechless,' I admitted, when she looked at me expectantly. Never, in my wildest dreams, had I thought she would have a turnaround like this, at the age of thirty-five, after having not touched magic for so long.

'I'm really happy for you, Raven,' I said, squeezing her hand reassuringly.

'Me too, Mum,' said Morgan. 'We can learn it all together.'

I smiled down at him.

'I'm going to take it slow,' Raven said. 'I'm not ready to reverse the binding spell... yet.'

'Do it when you're ready, Mum,' said Morgan. 'But, right now, we need to get back to this.' He pointed at the sword in his lap and I bent down to take a look. The blue enamel on the hilt was chipped away with age, and the blade itself was rusted and cracking.

'I found it in a chest under my bed,' Morgan said, sounding unsure. 'Will it be good enough?'

'It's perfect,' I reassured him. 'You won't actually be using it, anyway. It's just for show. Do you have the nullifying spell?'

I was feeling suddenly anxious. When I had come up with this idea, I had thought it was clever, maybe even a little funny. But now, I was wondering if we had gone to far. The spell was incredibly dangerous, and in the wrong hands it would mean disaster. I had to make sure that, from this moment forward, that sword didn't leave my sight.

'I have it,' said Frank, and he held up a small, thimble-sized bottle of black liquid. 'I have the Grimm spell, too.' He pulled Morgan's potion from his pocket.

'You do the honour, lad,' he said, handing the jar over to Morgan. I intercepted it and gently closed the wizard's hands back around the glass jar.

'No, Frank. You have to pour it over the sword during the games. Not a moment sooner,' I warned. 'And make sure you use the nullifying spell the moment the games end and the winner is announced, okay?'

Frank nodded and took the blade from Morgan.

LIFE'S A WITCH

'We need to go,' he said, looking out at the sun as the rays streamed through the window.
Yes, but I needed to change first.

Chapter 23

Walking into the throne room, wearing the robe Heston had made for me, somehow left me feeling more self-conscious than when I had arrived wearing my own patched-up clothes.

I could feel his eyes on me as I walked through the doors, and I could feel the weight of what accepting this gift might mean to him.

To me, it was just a pretty black dress that I wanted to wear.

It *was* very pretty, with constellations handsewn with silver thread, and straps that criss-crossed over my shoulders and back.

I had let my hair hang down and wild, but had allowed an attendant to twist diamond hair charms into it.

Next to me, Raven was a vision in a skin-tight purple gown. Beth wore a short black dress, with purple stockings and a black, studded belt. Finn stood a little away from us, maybe because he didn't want to be associated with our fashion choices. He looked good as always, in his adapted uniform. Morgan was wearing a suit, in a colour that matched that of his mother's. He had tried to gel his hair down flat, but instead it was now sticking up in odd, angled spikes.

Frank outshone us all, in bright blue robes. The bell sleeves trailed down to his feet, and the skirt of his robes had a long train that I accidently kept stepping on.

As we walked in, an attendant announced Frank as a challenger, which set the large crowd of guests to cheering and whistling.

The throne room was immaculate, as it was also the dual celebration of the ceremony end, and the Pumpkin Ball. Long tables were laid out with orange and gold settings. No food had been served yet, but there was already a small line of people waiting in anticipation.

Heston was standing on the dais, his gaze directly on us. Well… me. He was a vision in a low-cut suit of black and red florals. He had chains looped in his ears and a choker around his neck with a large emerald in the middle. There was no sign of the glass pendant, and I wondered if he had taken it off on purpose.

I reached to my own bare neck and smiled.

A loud clapping erupted around us then. My attention was drawn to the ring, where a young witch with a shaved head and heavy black eyeliner was pacing around, waving her arms and hyping up the crowd.

'Our contestants have all arrived,' announced an attendant. He was holding a large baton in his hand, and that was the only warning he gave before he bashed it against a brass gong that had been partially concealed by the crowd. I covered my ears as the sound reverbed around the room.

Frank walked over to the rope, and we all trailed behind.

Another attendant gestured for him to enter. I grabbed his arm.

'Are you ready?' I asked.

He nodded. 'I've done this several times before, you know,' he replied with a wink.

The witch growled at him as he stepped over and Frank chuckled.

'No need for that,' he said. 'Shall we let our magic do the talking?'

The witch spat at the floor where Frank stood. 'You won't beat me, old man. I have been working on this spell for years.'

'And I have had holidays that lasted longer than the entirety of your life span,' Frank replied, 'so I am not concerned.'

We needed to work on the smack talk a little.

Without any warning, the gong rang out again. The guests cheered and I grabbed hold of the rope anxiously.

'Ladies first?' asked Frank.

LIFE'S A WITCH

The witch said nothing. Instead, she pulled a small charm from out of her pocket.

'This is a spell of invisibility,' she announced, holding it up for all to see.

It was a thin, black twine of string with what looked like a red card attached.

'But it is not like any spell of invisibility you have known,' she continued. 'I will not just turn opaque. I will actually be invisible. My being will no longer exist on this plane. You will not be able to see me, you will not be able to touch me.'

A few people gasped in excitement. One man yelled, 'How much for it?'

'It's priceless,' the witch hissed. 'Would you like a demonstration?' she asked, turning to Frank.

'Yes, please,' Frank prompted, sounding quite enthusiastic himself.

The witch placed the charm around her neck and immediately disappeared.

'Try to touch me, if you can!' she dared Frank.

He stepped forward and waved and gestured around in the air, flapping his long dress robe frantically. He tossed his black and pink beard over his shoulder, and then began to kick out wildly, as if he was practising some form of fighting arts. Eventually, he stopped and clapped his hands together.

'That is a fine bit of witchcraft!' he announced. 'May I have the recipe for my books?'

I shook my head at the wizard. He wasn't supposed to be impressed by his opponent. The crowd seemed to find this endearing, however, and many laughed and jeered, or cried out for the witch to 'Give him the recipe!'

I chanced a glance at the dais to see that Heston was standing on the last step, watching intently with his arms crossed over his chest. His eyebrows were furrowed. I had to admit that he looked almost a little nervous.

I wondered if he was more concerned about Frank winning, or Frank losing.

The witch reappeared and many people clapped.

'Your turn, then, old man,' she said, after bowing at her fans.

Frank wasted no time at all. He pulled the decaying broadsword from out of his sleeve and waved it about in the air. A few people cheered at the sudden possibility of violence, but most looked upon the worthless sword with confusion.

Then, Frank unstoppered the potion in his other hand and poured the contents onto the blade. I flinched at the small splattering of pure black liquid that splashed to the floor. As the blade became saturated with the potion, it began to glow. Sparkling tendrils of emerald-green magic clamoured and crawled over the sword, merging and forming a beautiful casing. Frank held the sword up again. More people cheered this time at the sight of the restored sword.

'And what is that, then?' asked the witch nonchalantly, but she was nervously biting her bottom lip.

'This is the Grimm blade,' Frank said as he lowered it and pointed it towards the witch. 'Do you know the Grimm spell?' The witch shook her head and took a step back.

'Well, you don't need to worry about it,' said Frank. 'It couldn't do much harm to you… well, no more than a normal blade. However…' He swung the sword around and pointed it towards the dais, angling it so that it was in line with Heston, who stood, looking interested. 'It could kill a vampire easily, or any immortal thing. Just one scratch, is all it would take.' Heston's eyes flared, and he looked at me in surprise.

'How would we know that?' complained the witch.

'We could try it out,' Frank teased. The witch quickly shook her head.

'You don't want to test out my blade?' Frank said, mocking her. The witch shook her head again and looked around for support.

'I am sure we could find a vampire to volunteer?' Frank asked the crowd.

The witch scowled at him, then held up her right hand, a sign of forfeit.

I smiled to myself. I had counted on Frank's opponents being too afraid to appear treasonous.

The gamble had paid off.

'My next opponent, please!' Frank cried. A middle-aged warlock stepped over the velvet rope, his black robe tangling awkwardly for a moment.

'And what is your example of wizardry and witchcraft?' Frank asked pleasantly. The warlock looked around uneasily, before pulling a frog from his pocket.

'I... uh, I am going to turn this frog into a man,' he said.

A few people clapped, but not enthusiastically. The warlock cleared his throat.

'It's not easy, you know,' he continued, trying to justify his skill. 'People always talk about turning people into frogs, but turning them back is a whole other thing.'

'He's right, you know,' I said, speaking without meaning to. The warlock looked at me thankfully and Frank turned and mouthed 'What are you doing?' I shrugged. It was true. I had never got the hang of it, after years of trying.

The warlock pulled a large green frog from his pocket. It was covered in little bumps and dark green spots. I found myself thinking about how similar it was to Josh, my ex-boyfriend.

The warlock threw the frog up in the air suddenly and, as it came back down, he sprayed it with a spell from a little white spray bottle. The effect was instantaneous. The frog turned into a tall, completely naked man.

A naked man I recognised.

'Josh?!' I yelled, aghast.

Josh's face contorted into rage as he recognised me.

'Hedgehog!' he yelled. His voice was croaky and low, very similar to a frog, actually. 'You complete and utter bit—'

However, he didn't get to finish insulting me, because his body contorted before our eyes back into a frog. He let out a loud, obscene noise in protest.

The warlock dipped down to pick up the frog and placed it back in his pocket.

'It doesn't last very long, unfortunately,' he admitted. 'But I'm getting there.'

The room was silent for a few moments, waiting to see if the warlock would do anything else. He stood with his squirty bottle clutched in both hands, looking a little bit lost.

'I have a Grimm sword,' Frank said, waving the sword around a bit. 'So…'

'Oh, yes… sorry.' The warlock held his right hand up to forfeit. Cheers went up around the room, but people were a bit confused now.

'Does anyone else want to challenge me?' Frank roared.

There was silence.

'Then, I think I have won?' he asked the attendant with the gong. The attendant nodded.

Honestly, it was all a bit of a let-down. The crowd clapped and whistled, but their hearts didn't seem in it. I think they had all hoped the appearance of a sword would end in bloodshed.

The witch with the impressive disappearing spell was finding solace in a drink and a few people were comforting her. Even I had to admit that her display had been more exciting than Frank's. It got the job done, however, and soon enough Morgan was jumping the rope to shake Frank's hand.

Raven was at my side, yelling, 'You did it, you did it!'

Frank had won, so why did I feel so... off?

I guessed a part of me had enjoyed being the Royal witch and now it was all over.

'You will accept my job offer though, won't you, Hodge?' I shivered as Heston appeared next to me and whispered in my ear.

I met his gaze and opened my mouth to decline. But, I had to admit, I couldn't think of a reason not to.

Raven wanted to learn more magic. She could easily take over the shoppe on some days, leaving me to do as I pleased.

Heston looked at me, expectantly, his ruby eyes searching my face.

'I... might,' I said. He gave a mischievous smile.

'That is good enough for me... for now,' he said. 'After all, the bargain we made was for you to be at my call for as long as I live, Royal witch or not.' I rolled my eyes, but couldn't help returning his playful smile.

Then, turning to the crowd of people, he yelled loudly, so that I had to cover my ears.

'The wizardry and witchcraft games have come to a unanimous close! Frank is the winner!

Chapter 24

'Frankincense Heston Oaken, you have shown yourself to be more worthy and more talented than any in your class,' said Heston. 'As your reward, you may request a place in my household.'

Frank's middle name was Heston? I had no idea. So that meant Edward had named his only son after the man he loved.

'Thank you for this honour, my King,' said Frank. He unhooked the sword from his back and Heston jumped back in alarm. I laughed wickedly, unable to help myself.

'Maybe we should put that somewhere safe?' Heston said, shooting me a look of disapproval.

Frank handed the sword to the nearest attendant and asked them to put it away in the tower. They nodded and rushed off.

'I am honoured by this opportunity, my King,' he repeated, going down on one knee. 'I have thought long and hard about the job I would like to request.'

I went cold then, suddenly remembering that Frank had always wanted to be the Royal pharmacist. He had been cheated out of the job twice. Would he allow himself to lose out on that chance again? I gripped my athame tight under my sleeve, and chewed my lip anxiously. Why hadn't I thought of that before? Would Frank betray me at this point? We barely knew one another, after all. Why would he throw away his future plans for me?

'And what have you decided?' pressed Heston, as the silence stretched on to agonising lengths.

'I would like to ask for the role of Royal wizard.'

I let out the breath that I hadn't realised I had been holding and felt my whole body relax.

Thank the goddess.

'I was worried just then,' Morgan whispered in my ear.

'Me too,' I admitted, chuckling with relief.

'I won't pretend you were my first choice for the role,' Heston said, shooting me a playful glance. 'But I can see that you are the best choice. Congratulations, Royal wizard.'

Frank rose to great applause, though no one clapped harder or louder than I did. It felt like a huge weight had been lifted from my shoulders. Raven inched closer to me and gave me a tight squeeze.

'You're free now,' she said. 'It's your time.'

I wiped a tear from her cheek and hugged her back tightly. 'Thanks, sis.'

'The games are over, hopefully for a very long time!' Heston laughed, addressing the crowd.

'Long live the King!' came the deafening reply in unison.

'Long live the King!' I cried, feeling relieved to be able to enjoy this moment now, without the threat of being imprisoned here for ever.

'Let the Pumpkin Ball begin!' Heston declared and, with a clap of his hands, everything set in motion.

Attendants flooded the room, carrying silver trays of food, the smell of cinnamon, pumpkin and nutmeg making my mouth water. Long, sparkling orange banners unravelled from the ceiling. The lights faded to black, only to flare up again almost immediately, revealing an ocean of floating black candles above us. The orchestra started up with a lively melody and people began to dance.

I chuckled to myself as I saw a large, human-sized pumpkin bobbing up and down through the crowd. Kate sure had gone the extra mile.

Heston walked over to me and knocked his hand against mine. He looked at me questioningly as he took a hold of it.

'I know you aren't ready for a relationship with me,' he whispered. 'But I still don't want to let you go just yet.'

I smiled up at him as he brushed his lips along my knuckles.

'I don't think I could completely abandon you. Even if I tried,' I admitted.

'There is only one thing left then,' said Heston.

'Dance?' I asked.

'Before that.'

Chapter 25

Heston, Raven, Morgan, and I stood bunched all together on the tower room landing, watching in anticipation as Frank placed his hand on the square emerald in the phoenix's claw. Then, after a few moments of nervous silence, the marble creature began to glow, brighter and brighter, until it was blinding.

I covered my eyes, and tried to push away the odd feeling of loss that panged in my chest.

This was what I had wanted. The job was never meant to be mine. But, I had to admit, it was nice to be a part of something as wild as the Manor, to have been accepted by it and, in a way, it had bound me to Heston.

When the light finally dimmed, the phoenix was once again holding the same rounded blue gemstone that it had held before.

'Now you, boy,' Frank said, gesturing to Morgan.

'What?' Morgan and I asked in unison.

'Well, isn't it obvious?' cried the wizard. 'With magic as strong as that, this child needs to have a proper apprenticeship! I'll take him under my wing, and then maybe one day I might actually get to retire!'

I laughed nervously, and looked to Morgan, expecting him to disagree. However, to my surprise, he was beaming with happiness.

'Can I, Mum?' he asked Raven, looking hopeful. My sister bit her lip nervously, but it didn't take long for her to cave.

'I want you to be happy, Morgan. The decision is yours,' she said, dropping a quick kiss on top of her son's head. He brushed her away, embarrassed.

'You still have to go to school, though,' she warned.

Morgan hesitated for only a second longer, before reaching out and touching the phoenix. That same light blazed in my eyes, forcing them shut. When it had calmed down, I opened my eyes again, to see that there were now two stones, one in each claw. The wizard's blue gem, and a square-cut emerald, almost the exact twin to mine.

Raven and Morgan hugged and I patted the old wizard on the back. I felt a happiness and excitement for the future that I hadn't felt in a very long time. I could tell everyone here could feel it, too.

Downstairs, the Pumpkin Ball was in full swing. The aroma of cinnamon and cloves seeped up from the kitchens, smelling more inviting that ever, and I couldn't wait to get back down, and maybe share a dance with a certain king.

'Well,' said Heston, from behind us. His voice was trembling with overflowing emotion. 'I think you have a very interesting apprenticeship ahead of you, dear Morgan.'

'Why is that?' I asked, slightly alarmed by his tone. When he didn't immediately reply, we all turned back to look at him.

'Because, I am being betrayed,' he gasped out.

My stomach lurched and my mouth fell open in horror at the sight before me.

I screamed and lunged forwards, but it was too late.

Heston teetered, then fell backwards, his body seeming to fold in on itself as it disappeared down the tower steps in a swathe of black and gold.

Standing now in the spot Heston had just occupied, was Uncle Trevor, still holding the now blood-covered Grimm blade in his hands.

The very one Frank had spelled.

The very one he had just stabbed though Heston's chest.

For a moment, there was a shocked, terrified silence. We were all too stunned to process what had happened before us.

Then, Trevor broke out into a loud, deranged laugh.

He wiped the blade on his cape and dropped the sword to the ground. It was useless now the spell had done its work, as all my spells did.

'So,' Trevor said, jovially, 'will someone be kind enough to go down and fetch me my crown from my dear, dead nephew's body?'

TO BE CONTINUED...

LIFE'S A WITCH

The Witches of Broome Hill will be back soon.

Hedgehog
Raven
Morgan
Granny Broome

SIMONE NATALIE

Simone Natalie lives in a little English town with her Husband, three boys, and a plant eating cat named Nova. She has been burying her head in books since before she could read them, and writing since before she could spell (That one is still fairly tricky, actually)

You can find Simone on Amazon, Facebook, TikTok and Instagram.

LIFE'S A WITCH

Out Now!

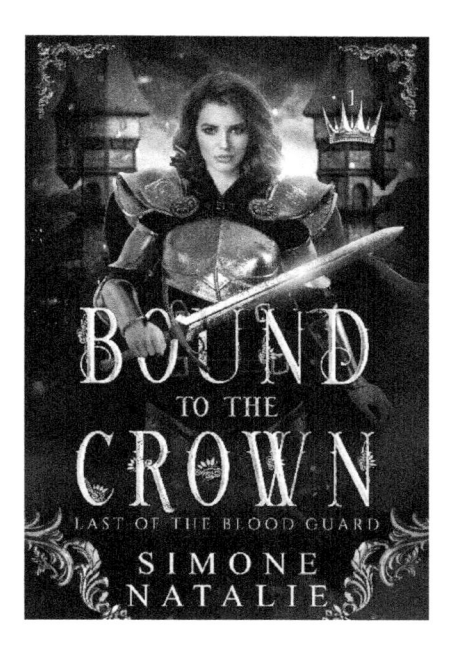

Enter a dark fantasy world full of corrupt knights, powerful witches, and nightmarish rulers, where one woman is forced to make the impossible choice between losing the people she loves the most and losing her own free will.

SIMONE NATALIE

*I am a **coward**.*
*I am a **murderer** and a **betrayer**.*

After six long years on the run, I have the chance to put right what I have done wrong and bury the past that haunts my dreams.

Do I take this chance, or do I value my life and keep running?

Cera is a renter girl at Madam Fredericka's work-house. She takes on any job that needs doing, from digging graves to pulling pints at the local pub. She works hard, keeps her head down, and never overstays her welcome. However, when Cera is tricked into helping a queen in distress she finds herself faced with the one thing she has been trying all these years to avoid—her past.

Stuck between an ex-boyfriend who wants her dead and a queen completely in over her head, Cera has to navigate her way to redemption without anyone finding out her real identity.

Bound to the Crown **is the first book in the highly-anticipated series** *Last of the Blood Guard.*

Printed in Great Britain
by Amazon